W

## Big Trouble

The cowtown of Concho was rife with lawlessness before Deputy Sheriff Cleve Stafford showed up with a clear order from the county sheriff: clean up the town and stop the rustling. The deputy expected big trouble and it was waiting for him the moment he showed his face in the main street. However, when the shooting started, it seemed that the gun was stuck in his hand and even when his three gun pards showed up to help he found the going tough.

Despite this, Cleve vowed he would succeed in his mission even though the lawless factions of the town was determined to beat the law.

Flaming guns and hard action were all Cleve could expect and his life was on the line.

*By the same author:*

Range Grab
Bank Raid
Range Wolves
Gun Talk
Violent Trail
Lone Hand
Gunsmoke Justice

# Big Trouble

CORBA SUNMAN

A Black Horse Western

ROBERT HALE · LONDON

© Corba Sunman 2001
First published in Great Britain 2001

ISBN 0 7090 7004 7

Robert Hale Limited
Clerkenwell House
Clerkenwell Green
London EC1R 0HT

Typeset by
Derek Doyle & Associates, Liverpool.
Printed and bound in Great Britain by
Antony Rowe Limited, Wiltshire.

# ONE

Cleve Stafford rode out of the high ground with the smell of hill pines sharp in his nostrils. He reined in and stepped down from the saddle, dropping his reins as he tried to rid his bones of the ache of travelling. Below him lay the single street of Concho, marked only by a series of well-spaced lanterns gleaming like yellow oases in the darkness. Concho was the second largest cowtown in Benson County, Kansas.

He sighed heavily, shrugging each shoulder in turn, then swung his arms before stamping around his horse to get the kinks, brought on by long riding, out of his body. The darkness pressed in around him, black and impenetrable, unrelieved by the dim light shed from the star-studded sky. He eased the cartridge belt encircling his slender hips, and unconsciously reached for the flared butt of the big pistol ensconced in the leather holster on his right thigh.

Incisive thoughts ran unchecked through his mind as he gazed into the darkness at the glimmering lights of the distant town. It had taken him four days to get to this spot from Whiskey River, the county seat, and he touched the silver deputy sheriff star pinned to his leather vest. There was big trouble in Concho, so he had been told, and he was on his way to deal with it. Sheriff Arlen, back in Whiskey River, had given him a free hand, and he had been wondering, over the past four days, how to proceed; although he figured it would be better to play his cards as they fell.

He climbed back into the saddle and continued, a big man for all his shapelessness in the close darkness. The sorrel snorted, moving with renewed vigour towards the string of lights below, for they held the promise of a cosy stable, feed and rest. The ground fell away from them in a long, gentle decline, making travel that much easier, and they splashed through a wide creek before arriving on the threshold of the only street of Concho.

Closer to the town, the light of the street lanterns was bolstered by dozens of lighted windows, and there was noise in many forms as he clopped through the dust, looking for the livery barn. A piano rattled out a boisterous tune as he passed the batwings of a saloon. There were high-pitched yells, coarse laughter, shouts and curses, and, somewhere, a woman screamed in a high vent of fear which was suddenly cut off. Two shots blasted quickly, punctuating the endless roll of noise with their raucous thunder.

Stafford sat straight in his saddle, eyes missing

nothing as he traversed the street. He had been warned that Concho was a hell town and he could not expect help in any form from its inhabitants, either lawful or unlawful. He passed three more saloons, and was aware that the shadowed side-walks were alive with pleasure-seekers, thronging the dusty boards.

He noted four horses tied to a hitching rail in front of the darkened bank and wondered why, at this time of the evening, the animals were not in the livery barn. Then he caught a glimpse of furtive light inside the bank, furtive because it flared and died swiftly, as if someone had instantly covered its source.

Before he could move further, a powerful blast thundered through the bank, blotting out the minor sounds emanating from the town. The blast thrust at Stafford, his sorrel rearing in fright. Stafford leapt from his saddle, twisting like a cat to land on his feet. He heard shattered glass tinkling as the echoes faded, and palmed his gun despite being dazed by the explosion.

Smoke and powder fumes were issuing from the shattered front window of the bank. Shaking his head, Stafford ran on to the sidewalk, cocking his gun, covering the opening door of the bank as his boots clattered on the boards. A six-gun flamed in the darkness of the doorway, cutting through the dense shadows with fiery brilliance.

Stafford returned fire as hot lead crackled past him. He dropped to one knee, aiming his pistol at the indistinct figures spilling out of the smoking building. A bullet tore through the wide brim of his Stetson. Another plucked at the folds of his neckerchief. But he ignored the danger as he took on the robbers.

The long-barrelled .45 bucked in his hand. Gunsmoke blew into his face. The two leading figures did not get past the doorway. Both went sprawling under the scourge of hot lead. The third figure paused in the doorway to exchange shots, and Stafford's probing lead tore out his throat. The fourth figure ducked back into the cover of the bank after sending two desperate shots in Stafford's general direction.

Stafford pushed himself upright. His ears were ringing with gun thunder. Echoes were rolling away across the town. The stench of burned powder was acrid in his nostrils. He broke his gun and fed fresh shells into the smoking weapon from the loops of his cartridge belt. Closing the weapon, he went forward, gun ready in his right hand, his reflexes hair triggered.

The three men sprawled in the doorway of the bank were inert, barely showing in the dense shadows. With his gun poised for further action, Stafford toed each of them in turn, and found no response. He blinked rapidly against the foul smoke pouring out of the shattered building, then went forward into the bank, hurling himself to the right and pushing his back against the inside wall.

A gun flashed from across the smoke-filled room

and a bullet plunked into the wall a scant inch from Stafford's left shoulder. He fired instantly in reply, and heard a sharp cry hard on the heels of the shot. Then a body thudded to the floor, and he exhaled deeply, almost choking on the thick fumes caused by the explosion.

Crossing the long room, he covered the inert figure as he bent to check it out. His probing fingers found a sticky patch on the man's chest, and he grasped a handful of shirt front and dragged the body towards the door, dropping it atop the tangle of bodies already lying there. He staggered out into the fresh air, gasping for breath, his nose wrinkled against the biting reek of black powder.

'Hold it right there!' A harsh voice snarled at him from the shadows to the right. Stafford froze and remained motionless. 'Get rid of your gun and don't do anything with your hands,' the voice continued. 'I got you covered. This is the law. Do like I say or you're dead.'

'Boone Hickey?' Stafford demanded.

'That's me. Don't move.'

'I'm Cleve Stafford, Hickey. Sheriff Arlen must have notified you about me.'

'Stafford! What in hell are you doing in the bank?'

'I was passing when the explosion occurred. I guess it put me in the right place at the right time. Far as I can tell, there were four robbers, and I got 'em lying in a heap here. Come forward and check them out.'

The shadows moved and a big figure materialized

from the darkness. Starlight glinted on a gun in
Hickey's right hand. He came to within a couple of
feet of Stafford, who was holding his gun down at his
side. The sound of boots on the boardwalk increased
as townsmen came hurrying excitedly to the source
of the explosion. Hickey yelled at the unseen
newcomers.

'Someone get a lantern so we can see what we've
got here,' he rapped. 'All of you, stay back and keep
quiet or there'll be hell to pay. The bank's been
robbed and four men have been shot, so keep your
long noses out of this.'

Stafford stood motionless, breathing easily.
Someone took a lighted lantern from a nearby
awning post and came forward with it, holding it
shoulder high to cast yellow light over the grim
scene. Hickey bent over the fallen robbers, dragging
them out of the doorway and placing them in an
orderly row on the sidewalk. He checked each one as
he did so, and when the fourth robber was clear of
the building he straightened and looked at Stafford.

'Hell, you killed all four of them! You sure didn't
waste any lead. So you're Cleve Stafford, huh?' His
probing gaze caught a glint of the law star on
Stafford's shirt front. 'I heard tell of you. A johnny-
come-lately who rode into Whiskey River a few
months ago with a reputation in law-dealing, and
made a big impression on Sheriff Arlen. The sheriff
made you Chief Deputy, so I heard, and now he's
sent you here to clean up Concho.'

'Someone's got to do it. ' Stafford holstered his gun

with a slick movement. 'You haven't done anything in the time you've been here, Hickey, and now I've arrived you're to go back to Whiskey River. Arlen wants you where he can keep an eye on you.'

'What's that supposed to mean?' Bluster filled the big deputy's harsh voice. He was several inches over six feet in height, and built like the side of a barn. He holstered his gun, clenched his right hand into a massive fist, and slammed it into the palm of his left hand, anger mingling with envy because of the rumours he had heard about this big newcomer.

'I reckon it means you ain't been pulling your weight around here,' Stafford said in a flat tone. Although Hickey was overly tall, Stafford found himself looking into the deputy's eyes from a similar height. 'You're to ride out for Whiskey River soon as I take over.'

'Has the bank been robbed?' A short, fat, well-dressed man pushed forward through the gathering crowd. He was dressed in a store suit and wore no hat. A drawn six-gun was clutched in his podgy right hand.

'Who are you?' Stafford demanded.

'August Hoffmeyer. I own the bank.' He was looking down at the four dead men, and hastily stepped over them to grab up two bulging cloth money bags lying in the doorway. 'This is the bank's money. Did any of the robbers get away?'

'No.' Stafford shook his head. 'Stand where you are, Hoffmeyer. Those two bags are evidence. Hickey, take a close look at the robbers and see if you can

put names to them. I want to wrap this up quick. I
need to get supper before the eating house closes. In
fact, you better take over here while I take care of
my horse and settle in. I'll see you at the law office
in about thirty minutes.'

'The hell I will! If my orders are to ride back to
Whiskey River the minute you get here then you can
do your own dirty work.' Hickey spoke harshly. 'I'm
finished with Concho as of this minute. Come along
to the law office and I'll hand over to you. You're
welcome to this godforsaken hole. Just see how you
get along with the folks around here. There ain't one
of them will hold out a hand to you, and no one is
prepared to back the law. I'm glad you're here,
Stafford. And I'll be interested to see how you make
out on your own.'

He turned on his heel and went off along the
sidewalk, pushing roughly through the crowd.

'Looks like you've hurt old Hickey's feelings,'
Hoffmeyer said. 'And good riddance to him. He
wasn't any good as a lawman. He allowed too many
rowdies to hang out in town. You're gonna have your
work cut out trying to restore order in Concho.'

'Maybe.' Stafford glanced sideways as a tall, thin
man pushed forward from the crowd. 'Who are you,
and what do you want?' he demanded.

'I'm Frank Willard, the undertaker. You'll need me
to take care of these bodies.'

'Yeah.' Stafford nodded. 'Get them off the street
soon as you can. Let's take a look inside the bank,
Hoffmeyer, and check the extent of the damage. You

can't wander around town with two bags of cash in your hands. From what I've heard of the situation around here, you'd soon be penniless.'

Hoffmeyer led the way into the bank. He dumped the money bags on a counter and went around lighting lamps. Fumes were still thick inside the building, and Stafford tried to breathe lightly to save his lungs. He looked around and saw a big safe in a corner, its thick door hanging open. Account books and miscellaneous papers were strewn on the floor, blackened and scorched. An inner door of the building was twisted out of shape by the effects of the blast.

'Looks like they used too much dynamite,' Stafford observed.

'They didn't touch the smaller safe.' Hoffmeyer produced a big key and went to the iron safe in question, opening it and hastily thrusting the money bags inside. There was a satisfied grin on his fleshy lips as he relocked the safe. 'I better get Tom Burns, the carpenter, to come and make the place safe. Those robbers sure made a mess of it. Thanks for stopping the robbery, Stafford. It's about time the law was strengthened around here.'

'There will be some changes, I can promise you that.' Stafford spoke firmly. He walked out to the sidewalk and looked around. There was a dense crowd now, clustered around the bodies of the robbers. Everyone was talking excitedly, but silence descended when Stafford appeared. 'You folks get back to what you were doing before the explosion,' he suggested. 'There's nothing more to see here. The action is over.'

Men began to drift away, and Stafford looked around for his horse. Someone had tethered the sorrel to a nearby hitching rail. He exhaled sharply to rid his lungs of the cloying reek of burned powder and went to the horse, grasping his reins and swinging into the saddle.

'Which way to the livery barn?' he demanded, and a dozen voices told him.

He rode along the street, his narrowed eyes probing the surrounding shadows. As he passed yet another saloon, three reeling cowpokes came blundering out of the building. Two of them were supporting the third, who drew his six-gun and fired five racketing shots at the stars. The trio fell to the sidewalk in a heap, and Stafford rode in close and stepped down from his saddle.

'What outfit are you?' he demanded roughly as the men made a concerted effort to regain their feet.

The men paused and gazed blearily at him, and the one who had fired the shots lifted the gun still dangling in his hand and began to line it up on Stafford. The big deputy stepped out of the line of fire and kicked out with his right foot. The toe of his dusty boot connected with the underside of the man's wrist and the gun went sailing from his grasp. He yelled in surprise and fell over flat on his back.

'What the hell!' One of the other two started to his feet, reaching for his holstered gun, and when he was erect he found himself staring into the muzzle of Stafford's levelled pistol, which was only an inch or two from the end of his nose.

'I asked a question,' Stafford rapped. 'Give me an answer. What outfit are you?'

'There's only one outfit that matters around here,' the man replied, 'and that's Big T.'

'What are you men doing in town in the middle of the week?'

'We was out hunting rustlers, and their tracks led close to town so we came in for a drink. We can't follow tracks at night. Who in hell are you? Boone Hickey is the only lawman in Concho.'

'Not any more, he ain't.' Stafford grasped the collar of the cowboy who had fired the shots and lifted him bodily to his feet. 'If you don't want to see the inside of the jail then you better get out of town and stay out. You got that?'

'You can't chase us out. We ain't done nothing wrong.'

Stafford thrust the drunken puncher against his sidekick and the pair sprawled across the sidewalk, feet moving rapidly as they tried to control their balance. The third puncher, in the act of rising unsteadily, impeded their progress and they all fell to the boards in a writhing heap.

'If I find you still in town when I've had my supper, I'll throw you in jail and lose the key for a few days,' Stafford rapped. He grasped one of the men and lifted him to his feet. 'Have you got that?' he demanded.

'We'll leave town,' the man replied grudgingly.

'Right now,' Stafford insisted.

'Yeah. Right now.' The man turned to help his sidekicks to their feet, and all three staggered back through the batwings into the saloon.

Stafford stifled an impulse to go after them, shaking his head as he turned away. He would attend to the finer details of law dealing when he had more time. But his expression was bleak as he returned to his horse and continued to the livery barn. Sheriff Arlen had briefed him on what to expect around here. Crookedness was rife in the town and on the range. Rustling was widespread, and the two foremost ranches, Big T and M Bar, were close to a range war because their owners blamed each other for the cattle stealing.

An old man came forward out of the shadows as Stafford dismounted in the doorway of the livery barn. A single lantern just inside the barn gave ineffectual light. Stafford handed his reins to the ostler.

'Grain him and water him slow,' he directed. 'He's come a far piece in the last four days.'

'So you're the new deputy, huh?' The oldster squinted at the glinting star on Stafford's chest. 'It would be too much to hope that you've come to replace Hickey.'

'I have, as a matter of fact.' Stafford took his saddlebags from behind the cantle of his saddle and slung them across his left shoulder, then slid his Winchester .44.40 out of the saddle boot. 'Hickey is finished around here as of now. Where's the nearest eating house?'

'Back along the street, on the left. But you'll have to hurry. I was in there a few minutes ago and they were fixing to close for the night. I'm Al Jory, and I'm glad to know you, Deputy. If there's any way I can help you then just let me know.'

'Thanks. I'm Cleve Stafford.'

The reddish flash of a gunshot tore through the shadows to the right, and Stafford ducked as a slug plunked into the front wall of the barn, just missing the crown of his Stetson. He dropped flat instantly, saddlebags falling from his shoulder. Thrusting his rifle forward, he sent three shots in reply, bracketing the area around the flash, and the noise of the shooting blasted across the town in slowly decreasing echoes.

Stafford sprang to his feet and ran to the left in a half-circle, muscles tensed for more shooting, but there was no reaction to his move. He uncocked the rifle and transferred it to his left hand. Palming his Colt as he closed in on the spot from which the shot had been fired, he moved cautiously, tense inside. His right foot found a discarded pistol and then he saw the body of a man lying beside the front corner of the barn.

'Bring a light,' he rapped, and the stableman appeared from inside the barn with a lantern. Stafford averted his gaze, watching the fallen man until the ostler arrived with the light. 'Do you know him?' he demanded when yellow light fell upon the upturned face of the dead man.

'Yeah.' The ostler spoke reluctantly. 'He's Dave

Pickett. Odd-job man around town. Drifted in some months ago, and always drank away every red cent he earned. Used to hang out in Griff Polder's saloon. He slept in a back room there.'

'Why would he want to take a shot at me?'

'He might have answered that if you hadn't killed him.'

'Yeah. Well there was no time to aim properly.' Stafford bent and searched the pockets of the dead man, and his gaze narrowed when he found a twenty dollar coin in a breast pocket.

'Jeez!' the ostler gasped. 'Where in hell would Pickett get that kind of dough?'

'It ain't much if he collected it for shooting me,' Stafford replied. He dropped the coin into his breast pocket. 'Take care of my horse and then fetch the undertaker. Tell him I said for him to take care of the body. I need to get me some grub.'

He collected his saddlebags and walked back along the street, crossing it at an angle, making for the left-hand sidewalk. His thoughts were grim as he continued. His arrival in town had been fortunate for the law. But it was obvious that Sheriff Arlen had not understated the bad situation existing here. He would have his work cut out to handle his job properly.

The door of the eating house was locked when he tried it, and he peered through a window and saw a woman placing chairs on the tables while a man mopped around the floor. He knocked loudly. The man looked up and waved a hand, indicating that the place was closed. Stafford knocked even louder and the man threw down the mop, his lips moving in a string of curses as he came to unlock the door.

'What in hell!' The man, dressed in a stained white apron, was short and fleshy, in his fifties and unkempt-looking. He seemed to be in a bad mood. 'Can't you see we're closed? I ve been open since six this morning. Whaddya want us to be, open twenty-four hours a day?'

'I just hit town and I ain't eaten since breakfast,' Stafford said easily. 'I got a lot of work to do between now and sun-up. Just give me something to keep me going, huh?'

'Mebbe you don't understand my language, huh? Just watch my lips. I said we're closed.'

'Is there another eating house in town?' Stafford's tone was deceptively friendly.

'Nope. This is the only one.' The man studied Stafford from under lowered eyelids, regarding the law star furtively, and sight of the law badge did not ease his hostility.

'You don't like the law?' Stafford demanded.

'Not the kind Boone Hickey runs around here.' The man chuckled as if he had made a joke.

'If you're not blind you'll see that I'm not Hickey. And I've just ordered him to get out of town. He's on his way back to Whiskey River as of now. I'm taking over in Concho.'

'Was that you making all the noise a few minutes ago? What was all the shooting?'

'I was responsible for some of it.' Stafford smiled

grimly. 'But I came out ahead of the others.'

'Well you better come in and take a seat. I can rustle you up some grub this time, but don't make a habit of dropping in here after we're closed.' The man turned and called to the waitress. 'Rosie, get some of the grub we were fixing to eat and bring it for this deputy. I'm Bob Carmody, Deputy, and I wouldn't let you in now if I didn't have an agreement to supply the prisoners in jail with their grub.'

'Thanks.' Stafford shook his head. 'I appreciate the gesture. When I get settled in around here you'll be supplying jail grub for half the men in town, I shouldn't wonder. You and me will have to work together, Carmody.'

The café owner grunted and returned to his mopping. Stafford sat down at a table and tried to relax. But he figured that the next few hours would be fraught with action and danger when he began to impose his will on Concho's lawless element.

# TWO

After eating, Stafford went along the sidewalk, rubbing shoulders with men who were out sampling the pleasures of Concho's nightlife. Several times he heard gunshots from around the town, and once a group of six riders galloped along the street, heading for out of town and firing pistols into the air as they went.

'Damnfool punchers!' someone growled beside Stafford after several slugs had smashed into the front of the building where they were standing. 'It's about time something was done about them. Three men have been killed already this week by stray lead. It ain't safe to set foot out here after dark.'

'What outfit are they?' Stafford demanded of the man who had made the remark.

'Heck, I didn't get a good look at them,' came the instant reply. 'And if I did I wouldn't go spouting their names around. You must be a stranger around here if you figure folks would be stupid enough to open their mouths.'

Stafford grimaced and went on to shoulder his way through the batwings of the next saloon he came to. The place was crowded with pleasure seekers. There was a long bar on the right which was crowded two-deep with drinkers. Half a dozen gambling tables were overflowing with men trying to buck the talents of house-gamblers, and a number of scantily-dressed saloon girls were mingling with the customers. A piano player was thumping out a tune in a corner.

The din made by the men present was deafening, and Stafford turned to leave, aware that he would be hard pushed to get a drink in peace. As he turned back to the batwings an immaculately-dressed man stepped in front of him, dressed in a smart store suit, boiled white shirt and a black string tie. Tall and slim, and looking every inch a gambler, he possessed a pair of inordinately wide shoulders, and looked to be a hard case despite his fine clothes and professional manner. He was well into his thirties, well groomed, with handsome features and slicked-down black hair.

'Howdy?' he greeted, eyeing the law star on Stafford's shirt. 'You'll be the new deputy I heard about. Welcome to my saloon. I'm Griff Polder, and if there's anything I can do for you then just let me know. Would you like a drink?'

'I just gave up the idea of getting one in here.' Stafford spoke ruefully. 'I'm Cleve Stafford. Looks like business is booming.' He was recalling what Sheriff Arlen had told him about Griff Polder. The man should not be trusted.

'Come into my office and we'll have a quiet drink,' Polder offered. 'Mebbe you've got the time to listen to one or two things I got on my mind.'

'Thanks, but I don't have time to spare at the moment. I got some business to sort out. Maybe some other time, huh?'

'Sure thing. I want you to know that I'm on the side of law and order. You can count on me, Cleve. It would be in my best interests to work with you. This town is pretty lawless right now. I heard what you did at the bank. It's about time the law was beefed up in these parts. And you've started off right by giving Hickey his marching orders.'

Stafford nodded. 'You'll see other changes around here,' he promised. 'By the way, do you know a man by the name of Dave Pickett?'

'Pickett?' Polder's dark eyes blinked a couple of times as he paused to consider. Then he nodded. 'Yeah. Pickett does odd jobs for me. Like he does for most businessmen around town, I guess. He's a drinker, too. Spends most of what he earns on the hard stuff. He hasn't come up against you, has he?'

'He did. Shot at me from cover. I had to kill him. Someone recently paid him a twenty-dollar coin. It was still in his pocket. You got any idea who wants to get rid of me?'

Polder shook his head. 'That's bad news. You're gonna have to watch your back after this, huh?'

'I'll be watching.' Stafford eased his saddle bags on his shoulder, hefted his rifle in his left hand, and moved on to the batwings. He went out into the darkness, stepping quickly into the surrounding shadows, then walked along the boards to the law office.

Boone Hickey was in the shabby office, sitting at the desk and leaning back in the chair, which was tilted on to its back legs. His boots were up on the desk. He was talking earnestly to a tall, solid look-ing man who seemed to be as broad as he was tall. Dressed in well-made range clothes, and wearing a wide-brimmed white Stetson, the man looked to be a cut above the average cowpoke. He glanced over his shoulder when he heard Stafford entering the office, and his slitted eyes narrowed even more when he took in Stafford's big figure and the glinting law badge on his chest.

'We was just talking about you,' he said as Hickey eased the front legs of his chair to the floor and removed his feet from the desk top. 'I'm Ben Tudman, owner of the Big T ranch. I've been waiting to see you.'

'I'm Cleve Stafford. Glad to know you, Tudman. Seeing you here saves me a ride out of town. I need to talk to you.'

'You got problems?' Tudman shook his head. He had blue eyes set deep in a rugged face, and his expression suggested that he was a man with many troubles. 'I thought I was the only one around here with problems. You want I should listen to you or will you let me get my stuff off my chest?'

'I can sort out my problems.' Stafford smiled. 'Tell me, what's bothering you?'

'Rustlers. I lost three hundred head of prime stock off my eastern range last night.'

'I'll look into it soon as I get settled in around here.' Stafford dumped his saddle bags on the desk and leaned his rifle in the nearest corner. 'You ain't left for Whiskey River yet,' he said pointedly to Hickey, who was gazing sullenly at him. 'What's keeping you?'

'I'm waiting to hand over to you,' Hickey growled. 'Don't worry, I'll be out of here before midnight.'

'Anyone in the cells?' Stafford pushed his hat to the back of his head, revealing a shock of curly black hair. His face was rugged, tanned by the outdoor life he had led. Standing three inches over six feet, he was perfectly proportioned, muscular, and oozing confidence. His blue eyes contained a shrewdness that indicated high intelligence.

'The cells are empty.' Hickey shook his head. 'It's a waste of time jailing malefactors. They get turned loose by Alford Ward, the lawyer, almost as fast as I lock them up. But that's your problem now. Sheriff Arlen figures you're a smart lawman, so we'll see just how good you really are when the chips are down. There are the cell keys, and I guess you know all about filling in reports and keeping the books. I'm gonna make tracks now, and I hope I never see the sky over Concho again.'

He hitched up his sagging gunbelt and strode to the door. Stafford watched him depart, shaking his head slowly as he recalled what Sheriff Arlen had said about Hickey.

'What about my rustled stock?' Tudman demanded.

'I'll look into the matter soon as I get time. I need to do something about the town before I can turn my attention to the range. Which brings me to the issue I want to take up with you. A short time ago I came across three of your men along the street. They came out of a saloon, all of them drunk, and one of them fired his gun at the sky. The details don't matter now. What I want is for you to tell your outfit that the town is off limits to all armed men, starting from the moment I can get notices printed and displayed.'

'I ain't about to tell my crew what to do when they're off duty.' Tudman shook his head emphatically. 'You take care of that chore yourself, if you think you can handle it.'

'I can handle it. I was thinking that there wouldn't be any bloodshed if you told them.'

'And what about the other cowspreads around here? Are you gonna hit them with the same law?'

'What makes you think I've singled out Big T for special attention?' Stafford grinned. 'From what I've seen of the town this evening, the law will go for every man carrying a gun inside of town limits.'

'You'll never make that stick.' Tudman shook his head. 'The jail ain't big enough, for one thing. You'd have fifty men in here inside of an hour.'

'Sure, if that's what it takes. I'm gonna start as I mean to go on. I've been told to clean up around here, and that's what I'll do. Have you any suspicion of who's stealing your cows?'

'Hell, if I knew that I'd have done something about them instead of coming in here wasting my time.' Tudman shook his head. 'I'll give you a coupla days to settle in, then I'll expect you to do something about the rustlers. I'll talk to my three men. They shouldn't have been in town, anyway. They were tracking some of the rustlers. If I find them in town I'll fire them. I run a tough crew, and I expect them to do what they're paid for.'

Stafford watched the rancher depart, then picked up the large bunch of keys and inspected the jail, finding room for a dozen prisoners in the cells. He took the keys with him when he departed, locking the street door at his back. Walking back along the street, he found the newspaper office and entered.

A printing press was being operated in the background by an old, white-haired man. There was a middle-aged woman seated at a desk in the foreground, and she looked up disapprovingly when Stafford entered. But her expression changed when she saw the law star pinned to his shirt front.

'You're the new deputy,' she said.

'Cleve Stafford, ma'am. I need some notices printed.'

'I'm Nella Harper, and that's Tom, my husband, doing the printing back there. How many copies do you need?'

'Fifty should do. And I'd like them soon as possible.'

She handed him a pencil and pushed a notebook towards him. 'If you'll write down what you want in the notice, I'll see that it gets done tomorrow.'

'Sure.' Stafford thought for a moment, then wrote a terse message explaining that it would be an offence for anyone to carry a gun within town limits, starting at noon the next day. He returned the notebook to the woman, watched her read the message, and saw a frown appear on her wrinkled face.

'This has been tried before,' she said, 'and it was an abject failure. That was in Deputy Tom Morgan's time. He was shot dead within hours of the notices being posted around town. It was unfortunate for the town that Boone Hickey was appointed after Morgan. Hickey did nothing for the law or the town.'

'I aim to change the image of the law in Concho,' Stafford said. 'Can I have the posters by dawn tomorrow?'

'I'll see what I can do. I wish you luck, Deputy. You're certainly going to need it.'

'Send your bill to the law office,' Stafford said. 'I'll call for the notices first thing in the morning.' He touched a forefinger to the brim of his hat and departed.

Making a round of the town without incident, he entered the saloon where the trio of drunken Big T riders had been drinking, and pulled up short on the threshold. Ben Tudman was standing at the bar, confronting his three men, who were even more drunk than when Stafford had seen them earlier. Tudman was shouting angrily, and one of the men was grasping the butt of his holstered gun.

'I ain't taking that kind of talk from you, Boss,'

the cowpoke was saying. 'We trailed those rustlers until it got dark and we couldn't see tracks no more. So we came in here for a little fun, meaning to pick up tracks again in the morning. There ain't no harm in that, and you got no cause to sound off at us. We ain't deserted our jobs. It was plain good sense to come in here for the night, the town bein' so close.'

'I pay your wages and I expect you to follow my orders,' Tudman thundered. 'You made a mistake coming in here, and added to it by disturbing the peace. The new deputy ain't a man to tangle with, and I don't want trouble with the law department. Now get your broncs and pull out of here back to the range, and be ready to resume the trail at dawn. If I get any more trouble from you then you can find other jobs, because you'll be finished at Big T. I won't employ men who can't obey orders.'

The three cowpokes backed off and came towards the door, gazing at Stafford's impassive face as they passed through the batwings. Moments later the sound of their horses leaving came to Stafford's ears, and he went to Tudman's side.

'I've done your dirty work,' Tudman said harshly. 'And you'll be doing me a favour by letting me know if my outfit steps out of line around here. If you're gonna make the law work then I'll help you where I can.'

'Thanks.' Stafford looked sideways at a man who came forward to greet Tudman. The newcomer was in his fifties, grey-haired, and dressed in a smart store suit. There was a swagger in his movements which Stafford did not miss.

'I'm glad you're keeping your crew in order, Ben,' the man said easily. 'It's about time something was done about the way punchers hoorah the town. It's got so decent folks are afraid to walk on the street. With a new deputy in town, something's got to change.' He looked at Stafford. 'I'm glad to say that Sheriff Arlen thinks highly of you, Stafford. I'm Pete Boxall. I own the Mercantile, and I'm the mayor of Concho. I've been expecting you to show up, and I want you to know that the town council, under my guidance, will co-operate with you any way we can. We need strong law-dealing around here.'

'Glad to know you, Mr Boxall,' Stafford nodded. 'You can start helping me by getting a by-law passed making it an offence for anyone to carry a gun within town limits.'

'There's one in effect already. We brought it in when Tom Morgan was deputy sheriff here. Morgan was keen to clear guns out of town, but he didn't last long enough to do anything about it. The law lapsed when Hickey took over.'

'I'll enforce it,' Stafford said firmly. 'But I'll need help. Why isn't there a town marshal?'

'Because no one will take the job, and we didn't cotton to the idea of bringing in a professional man. Some of those gunfighters are worse than the bad men they're hired to fight.'

'There are some good men around. I know a few of them.' Stafford nodded slowly. 'I could have one in particular here in town in a few days. He's between jobs right now. Finished taming a town over Denton way just last week, so I heard. I'll get in touch and invite him to come in and talk with you.'

'If you can recommend him then send for him right away,' Boxall said eagerly. 'I figure it's almost too late to make a stand against the local hard cases, but we have to make the effort or we'll always regret not doing so. You'll need more men though. I've seen this sort of thing tried before. Arlen should have sent more deputies with you. It'll take at least six of you, working day and night, to handle the lawlessness around here. It's deeply rooted now.'

There'll be three other deputies in here within two days,' Stafford said. 'I talked it over with the sheriff and he agreed with my ideas. I've come in first to get things moving, and I'll have gun-help very soon.'

'That's the best news I've heard in a long time,' Boxall said. 'I'll round up the rest of the town council right now and start things moving from my end. I'm glad to know you, Stafford. You just might be able to do what others before you have failed to accomplish. But we'll be behind you all the way. Excuse me now. I got things to do.'

Boxall hurried away, leaving the saloon, and Tudman grinned harshly as the batwings flapped behind the town mayor.

'You've lit a fire under him, Stafford. But I reckon the only thing that'll come out of this is your funeral. I'll back you though, until they put you down in the dust. Will you have a drink with me? I think I might not get the chance later to buy you one.'

Stafford smiled and shook his head. 'I don't drink when I'm on duty, and I'll be alone prowling around town until my help arrives. But thanks for the offer. I'll take you up on it later, if I'm still alive to collect. See you around, Tudman.'

He left the saloon and went along the sidewalk to check that Tudman's three drunken riders had really left town, and paused by the livery barn at the end of the street to consider the situation. The town had more than its usual share of rowdies and hard cases, and that in itself pointed to big trouble building up. But the reason for it eluded him at the moment. Someone was playing for high stakes, keeping behind the scenes while his plans came to fruition. It would be a case of waiting and watching while trying to put down the more flagrant excesses around the town.

The sound of a furtive footfall off to his left alerted him to the danger of standing alone in an unfrequented part of town. He slid sideways instinctively, palming his six-gun with practised ease, then dropped to one knee as his back touched the front wall of the barn. He was none too soon. In that instant a reddish flash of gunfire streaked the darkness nearby, and a bullet thunked into the woodwork beside him as Colt-fire blasted the silence.

Stafford returned fire immediately, spacing out three shots at the spot where muzzle flame had shattered the close darkness. He dropped flat and rolled to the left, coming up into the aim a yard from his original position. Two other guns had joined in the shooting and were hurling lead into the space he had vacated. He returned fire, aiming at gun flashes. His eyes were slitted against the gunsmoke flaring around him.

This was the hard way to deal the law, he knew, but he was ready to accommodate the badmen on all levels. It was his job to face troublemakers. His hammer clicked on a spent cartridge and he immediately changed position, reloading his weapon as he moved. But the shooting was evidently over, and an uneasy silence returned as gun echoes faded away.

Stafford got to his feet and moved along the face of the barn, until he was at an angle to the spot where the shooting had erupted. His eyes were accustomed to the shadows as he eased forward, gun uplifted and ready for action. His ears were strained to catch furtive sound.

There was a broken-down buggy a few yards out from the corner of the barn, and Stafford paused, eyes narrowed, to check it out. The shooting had come from that spot, and he made out the inert figure of one of the ambushers sprawled in the dust beside the wreck. But he was more interested in the other two guns that had fired at him and were still at large in the darkness.

The night breeze was blowing straight into his face, making his eyes water, and he blinked rapidly as he looked around, listening intently. There was no sound anywhere, but he had not heard his attackers departing. He eased down to one knee and felt around in the dust with his left hand, his searching fingers closing around a fist-size rock. Straightening, he hurled the rock at the buggy. It clattered loudly on the woodwork, evoking an immediate response. Two guns blazed furiously, and bullets slammed into the barn wall with powerful tearing sounds, just missing Stafford.

But he had already dropped flat, and returned fire as the deadly tattoo of striking lead flailed around him in the uncertain darkness. He felt the tug of a bullet passing through the upturned brim of his Stetson, and then experienced the lightning strike of lead ripping through his left sleeve just below the elbow, burning his forearm. He returned fire, teeth clenched and eyes narrowed.

One gun fell silent immediately, and Stafford pushed himself to one knee, aiming for the centre of a gun flash and triggering his gun without conscious thought. His ears were singing from the crash and thunder of the shooting, and his eyes were dazzled by the brilliant flashes that winked and died.

He held his fire when no further shots came at him, reloading his gun methodically, watching and listening for movement. When he heard the sound of boots approaching on the boardwalk as men came to investigate the shooting, he got to his feet and dusted himself down. A voice called to him from just inside the barn, and he turned quickly, levelling his gun.

'I think you got them all,' a man said. 'This is Al Jory, the liveryman. I watched your play from the start. The three men out by the buggy are Big T riders. I heard 'em talking about laying for you for getting them in bad with Ben Tudman. You showed up before I could get away from here to warn you. They were out to kill you, but I figure you nailed all three of them. I never saw better gun-work.'

'Bring out a lantern so I can take a look around here,' Stafford said harshly, and crouched, readying himself to continue the fight as the ostler emerged from the barn with a lantern. But he saw three inert bodies lying sprawled in the dust, and went forward to check on them as the foremost of the curious townsmen arrived.

Ben Tudman was leading the group, and the Big T rancher cursed angrily when he identified the men he had ordered out of town.

'I don't understand this,' he said furiously. 'My crew haven't been on the prod around here. They're all good, hardworking punchers, although they play hard. But I didn't have any of them pegged as killers. I don't employ such men. I leave that to M Bar, who have some mighty tough galoots on their payroll, but I doubt if even Charlie Martin would resort to tangling with the county law.'

Stafford did not reply. He had caught the sound of approaching hoofs coming in through the darkness of the trail and his fingers were busy checking his gun. When four riders loomed up out of the shadows he was ready for further trouble, holding his gun down at his side as the newcomers reined in before him.

'Talk of the devil,' Tudman muttered. 'Here's Charlie Martin and some of his M Bar outfit. This could be bad trouble for you, Deputy.'

# THREE

'What in hell is goin' on here?' demanded the foremost of the riders. 'We heard shooting. Who are those men down in the dust?' He kneed his horse forward a couple of paces and the animal's head would have struck Stafford's face if he had not stepped aside.

Stafford grasped the bridle of the horse with his left hand and pushed its head away. His right hand was holding his drawn gun. He saw the three riders in the background make swift movements towards their belts and warned them.

'Hold it right there,' he snapped. 'I'm Cleve Stafford, the new deputy sheriff. I'm running the law around here now. Don't make the mistake of pulling your irons, gents, or there'll be more dead men in the dust.'

He loosed his grip on the bridle of the horse and reached up for the rider, grabbing the man's belt and hauling him out of the saddle. The man was big, but could not resist Stafford's strength. He came out of the saddle with an involuntary cry of surprise but managed to kick his feet clear of the stirrups. He landed heavily in front of Stafford.

'I don't like having a horse thrust in my face,' Stafford rasped. 'I've a notion to teach you some manners. Charlie Martin of M Bar, huh? You figure to make big tracks, so I've heard. Well you don't stand taller than the law, Mister. You better back up or put up. I don't need to be side-tracked no how.'

'Why you—!' Martin slapped leather in his rage at being manhandled. 'Nobody lays a hand on me and gets away with it!'

Stafford blocked the rancher's draw with his left hand and slammed the long barrel of his pistol against the side of Martin's skull, just above the ear. The rancher's hat cushioned the blow, but it was powerful enough to drop him to his knees, where he knelt in a daze, shaking his head.

Stafford shifted his muzzle slightly to cover the three riders, who were again reaching for their guns. The three clicks of his weapon as he cocked it sounded ominous in the ensuing silence.

'I've warned you men not to touch your guns.' Impatience sounded in Stafford's voice. 'Now get your hands up where I can see them or you'll wind up as buzzard bait.'

The riders froze and lifted their hands shoulder high. Martin started to push himself to his feet, and Stafford snatched the pistol the man had drawn.

'You others, shuck your guns one at a time, and do

it slow,' he rapped, the muzzle of his pistol resting against Martin's breast bone.

'Do like he says,' Martin ordered. His voice was thick with suppressed fury, and his men disarmed themselves silently. 'I'm sorry, Stafford. I left my range in a temper because someone stole a big herd of my beef, and I meant to make someone pay for that. I guess I should have known better than to come in on the prod and pick on the law. Boone Hickey ain't never been a good lawman, and when I saw your badge I figured you was another of his ilk.'

'Hickey should be long gone from town by now,' Stafford said. 'Come along to the law office and tell me about the rustling. You come as well, Tudman. Mebbe it's the same gang hitting both your outfits.'

'You lost stock, Tudman?' Martin demanded. 'Looks like this rustling business is coming to a head.'

'You've both lost stock before?' Stafford asked.

Both ranchers agreed, and Stafford suppressed a sigh.

'Why haven't you got together to try and beat this thing?' he demanded.

'I had a suspicion that M Bar could be responsible for my losses,' Tudman said sharply.

'What the hell! I been considering the same thing about you, Tudman,' Martin rapped. 'We found some tracks today showing that my stock crossed your line and headed north-east.'

'Is that so? If I stole your herd do you think I'd be

stupid enough to trail it across my own range?'
Tudman demanded.

'Cut it out!' Stafford ordered. 'You won't get
anywhere accusing each other. While you're fighting, the whole range could be cleaned out.'

'Heck, there's a lot of truth in that,' Tudman said.

'I guess there is,' Martin agreed. 'OK. I'm willing
to hold my fire until a proper investigation has been
made.'

'I'll go along with that,' Tudman agreed reluctantly.

'I'm glad you both do,' Stafford told them. 'I would
have jailed the pair of you if you hadn't. I've got my
hands full at the moment, trying to settle the town,
and that's got to be my first priority. When I've
handled that I'll give my full attention to your problems, so don't make the chore tougher for me than
it has to be by going off half-cocked about the
rustling.'

'If you need some guns to back your play in town
then my crew is at your disposal,' Martin said.

'Thanks, but I've got some men coming in shortly
and I'll rely on them. You can help by ordering your
men to shuck their guns before coming into town in
future. As of tomorrow I mean to enforce the law
about not carrying guns inside town limits.'

'Do you figure you can make that stick?' Martin
laughed harshly. 'Hell, there's so much lawlessness
in this county that a man would be helpless if he
didn't carry a gun.'

'What you do out on the range is your business,'

Stafford said firmly. 'But no one, except lawmen, will carry guns in town after today.'

'That was tried before, and the deputy in charge wound up dead.' Tudman's voice carried a sour note. 'You can't ask a man to disarm himself when there's so much violence going on. Rid the town of the hard cases before you pick on the cow spreads. I wouldn't be able to get my men to leave their guns behind, so it's no use asking.'

'I've told you what the law is, and any man found carrying a gun will be jailed and fined.' Stafford shook his head as he watched the undertaker and an assistant begin removing the bodies.

'I swear I don't know why those three laid for you,' Tudman said. 'They shouldn't have been in town, anyway.'

'Just don't let there be any more trouble around here.' Stafford turned away. 'I got work to do, and I'm dropping behind schedule. Come and talk to me tomorrow about your rustling losses.'

He left the two ranchers standing and went back along the street. Despite his outward appearance of confidence he was fraught with indecision, aware now that he should have had gun help from the moment he arrived in town. But he was alone, and it seemed that the whole town was against him.

He went back to the law office and stood in the centre of the room, looking around with a cynical gaze. Hickey had not even bothered to keep the place clean. He sat down at the desk and checked through the paperwork piled on its dusty surface.

There were several Wanted posters with descriptions of known outlaws, and he discovered that no bookwork had been done for weeks.

Outside, a gun crashed raucously. The big front window of the office shattered and a bullet ploughed into the back wall just above Stafford's head. He ducked and hurled himself to the floor as gun echoes sounded outside in the darkness. Landing on the rough boards on his left shoulder, he palmed his gun without conscious thought. Glass tinkled to the floor as he waited, and then a whole fusillade of shots blasted out of the silence. The office was filled with flying death as bullets plunked and thudded into the back wall, boring through furniture and hammering into objects.

When the lamp was struck and extinguished, Stafford crawled out from behind the desk, gun in hand. He kept his head down while the tumult lasted, and when the shooting ceased he got quickly to his feet and edged in close to the window, peering out into the darkness, looking for movement.

The shadows were dense across the street and he saw nothing. He went to the door and eased it open, stepping outside quickly and placing his back against the front wall of the office. Echoes were fading slowly, grumbling away across the town. His ears were ringing from the shock of the attack, and he breathed shallowly, his lungs irritated by dissipating gunsmoke.

The sound of rapidly departing hoofbeats sounded from the back lots beyond the far side of the street, and Stafford shook his head. There was no chance of catching the culprit, and he relaxed slightly, although his alertness did not falter. He heard boots thumping the sidewalk as townsmen came to check on the shooting, and turned to fade into the alley beside the jail, not wanting further useless talk about the attack. This was a time for action, not talk.

The alley was dark and he was on unfamiliar ground. He felt his way along to the far end and stood for a moment with a sharp breeze blowing into his face, wondering what would be his best course of action. There was not much he could do until daylight returned, for he was at a big disadvantage with shadows concealing his adversaries. But he had expected some opposition to his arrival. Having shown that he was determined to put down lawlessness in any form, he had set himself up directly against well-established crookedness, and those running the stealthy business were not prepared to let him succeed.

He walked slowly along the back lots, able to see and avoid some obstructions when his eyes became accustomed to the gloom. He reached the rear of the hotel and tried the back door. It was locked so he went along the alley to the street, and walked casually into the lobby via the front doorway. He was tired, and decided to call it a day.

The hotel clerk was seated behind the reception desk, reading a newspaper, and sprang to his feet when he looked up and saw the law badge on Stafford's shirt.

'What can I do for you?' he demanded.

'I need a room. One that's quiet.'

'How long do you reckon on staying?'

'That depends on those against me.' Stafford forced a mirthless laugh and turned to face the door as someone came into the lobby from the street.

'Heck!' the newcomer exclaimed. 'There's a man on the sidewalk by the store, with a knife in his chest.'

'Show me.' Stafford moved to the door.

The man turned and departed quickly. Stafford lengthened his stride to stay in touch, half expecting a trick. He tensed as he plunged out into the darkness after the man, suspecting another outbreak of shooting. But nothing happened, and he followed the man along the sidewalk to the front of the store, where a crowd was gathering around an inert figure sprawled on the rough boards.

'He's been robbed,' someone declared. 'It's Sam Wenn.'

'I heard a cry as I came out of the saloon,' said the man who had fetched Stafford. 'I didn't see anything, and almost fell over the body. This is the second mugging this week. When is the law gonna do something about these crimes? It ain't safe to walk the street after nightfall.'

Stafford bent over the body. Someone came up carrying a lantern, and yellow glare illuminated the grim scene. The dead man was covered in blood, the knife sticking out of his chest, having pierced his heart.

'Who is he?' Stafford demanded.

'Sam Wenn, who owned the lumber yard,' some-one volunteered. 'It's well known that Sam didn't trust the bank with his dough. He carried it around in a money belt.'

Stafford ran his hands over the still body. There was no money belt. He straightened and looked around at the unfamiliar faces surrounding him. For all he knew, the killer could be standing next to him.

'Does he have a family?' he asked, and half a dozen voices volunteered information. Sam Wenn was married and had two children. A tall man pushed through the growing crowd and confronted Stafford. The townsfolk eased back deferentially at the sight of him. 'Who are you?' Stafford demanded.

'Doc Wilson.' He bent over the corpse and straightened again almost immediately. 'Dead! Stabbed through the heart. Has anyone gone to inform Mrs Wenn?'

'The body was only discovered in the last couple of minutes,' Stafford said. 'Did anyone witness the attack?' He paused and looked around at the intent faces watching him, and, when there was no reply, he nodded slowly. 'That's what I figured. Nobody is gonna talk. Townsfolk are moving around the street like there will be no tomorrow, and Sam Wenn is knifed and robbed but nobody sees it happen. I reckon you've got a big job on hand around here, Doc. Everyone is blind.'

Doc Wilson shook his head. He was almost as tall as Stafford, but thin, round-shouldered and quite old. His lean features were more than half obscured by a bushy moustache. 'It ain't sensible in this town to talk to the law,' he said patiently. 'These folk have seen it done before, and witnessed the consequences. The bully boys around here are vicious. When they strike they kill. It ain't safe to use your eyes in Concho, or your mouth.'

'Can you put names to the bully boys?' Stafford demanded. 'I'd like to meet them.'

'You will before long,' Wilson prophesied, and laughed sardonically. 'You better be ready for them.'

Stafford nodded. 'Has someone notified the undertaker?' he asked, and turned away when there was no reply.

'I'll tell Willard about this,' Doc Wilson called after him. 'I'm the county coroner. I'll examine the body and let you know my findings.'

Stafford shook his head, keenly aware that he was on his own in the town. The honest men were afraid for their lives, and the only way he could get to grips with the bad men was by catching them in the act of breaking the law. He walked back to the hotel, where two travel-stained horses were standing at the hitch rail before it, and paused in the lobby when he saw two newcomers at the reception desk. Relief filled him when he recognized them. Howard Riley and Shemp Peck were two of the three assistants the sheriff had promised him to help in bringing law back to Concho. He had not been expecting them for another two days at least, but here they were in the flesh, and he went forward to greet them.

Everything about Howard Riley was larger than life. In his late twenties, he was taller than Stafford, heavily built and slab-muscled, with yellowish hair that showed untidily from under the brim of his battered, weatherbeaten black Stetson. His red-check shirt, a size too small, was strained over his solid figure, and there was a glinting deputy badge pinned to it. His face showed many signs of having been battered in the past. There were lumps and bumps around the eyes, mute testament to the tough career he had followed as a bare-knuckle fighter before enlisting to work for the law. His keen blue eyes peered steadily with a farseeing gaze, as if perpetually looking beyond the horizon for something that he could not see near at hand. He was wearing a pistol in a holster on his massive right hip, butt forward for a crossdraw. His large face was unshaven, covered in a mass of wiry black hair.

Shemp Peck was the exact opposite to his bigger companion. Aged somewhere in his middle thirties, he stood at least five inches below six feet and looked puny in comparison with Riley. Small boned and thin to the point of looking fleshless, the twin cartridge belts buckled tightly around his narrow waist seemed to weigh him down, and the flared handles of the two six-guns he wore seemed much too large for his small hands. His face was pinched, his lips thin and compressed, and his dark eyes were beady, like those of a vulture seeking prey.

'I'm glad to see you two,' Stafford said, and both men swung around to gaze at him. Riley grinned and stuck out a great paw of a hand. Peck merely nodded, watching as the two bigger men shook hands, his eyes dull and without interest, his manner remote.

'We was just getting the lowdown on what's been goin' on around here since you hit town, Cleve,' Riley boomed in a husky voice that seemed to originate from deep in his chest. 'You could have waited for us before starting work. Heck, you get all the fun. I'll bet you ain't left anything for us to get our teeth into. I'm a mite tired of picking up the pieces you leave when you've finished law dealing.'

'Whatever you've heard, you better believe that I haven't started yet,' Stafford replied. He looked at the smaller man, who had no inclination to make contact. 'How are you, Shemp? Say, you look like you've grown half an inch since I last saw you.'

Peck's small face became animated and he grinned. Then he sobered quickly and shook his head. 'Heck, you're joshing me, Cleve,' he accused. 'You know I'm past the age of growing. I'm stuck down here and I got to make the best of it. You big fellers have got it made all ways to the middle. What you got for us? Do we start work now or in the morning?'

'Now that you're here I figure we can get to it.' Stafford grinned. 'Before you showed up I was about to call it a day, but now we can mosey around the town and see if there's anyone out there who wants to buck the law. Where's Bill Harra? Didn't he ride in with you?'

'He sure did,' Riley boomed. 'But he came into town alone. He figures to work from the other side this time. Something he agreed with Sheriff Arlen. I'm to tell you to ignore Harra. He's gonna stick his nose into the same trough the bad men are using. Do you go for that, Cleve?'

'Looks like I'll have to, if the sheriff set it up,' Stafford shrugged. 'But I'm warning you. This is one tough town. Don't take any chances.'

'Will you gentlemen be requiring rooms?' the hotel clerk cut in.

'No,' Stafford decided. 'We'll use the jail as living quarters. That way we can stick together and be ready to back each other while the chips are down. Come on, I'll show you where the jail is.'

He led the way out to the street, and spurs tinkled musically as they strode along the sidewalk. When they reached the jail, glass crunched under their boots. Riley gazed at the broken front window of the office and uttered an exclamation.

'Wowee! You ain't far wrong when you say there's some tough galoots around here. Looks like we got here just right, Shemp. The sheriff has sure picked us a tough one this time. You got a line on any hard cases, Cleve? We could have some fun beating the sass out of them.'

'You'll get all the fun you need when we start in on the serious stuff.' Stafford entered the office. He turned up the lamp and they looked around at the bullet holes decorating the walls.

'Looks like they're playing for keeps,' Peck

decided, his hands resting on the butts of his twin guns. 'There must be some pretty big trouble around here, huh?'

'Some, but nothing we can't handle.' Stafford picked up the cell keys from the desk and led the way through to the cells. 'I figure we can bunk down back here,' he mused. 'We're gonna have to stick pretty close together until we get a line of who's causing all the trouble. Since I rode in there's been an attempt to rob the bank. I've been shot at from cover, and I've killed several men.'

'That ain't bad for your first day.' Laughter boomed from Riley's massive chest. 'Let's get our gear in here, and when we've taken care of our broncs we can go looking for trouble. There must be some guys around who'll wanta try their luck against us.'

'I'll fetch the horses,' Peck decided, and departed in a hurry.

'Sheriff Arlen said rustling is bad out on the range,' Riley observed. 'Are we gonna straighten out the town before we tackle the cow problem?'

'That's the way I figure it,' Stafford nodded. 'I already met two of the local ranchers. I had to kill three of Ben Tudman's Big T outfit, and then tangled with Chuck Martin of M Bar. Both men came into town to report cattle losses, and they're pretty sore about the rustling.'

'The sheriff said you're to give Polder some attention. He owns a saloon, and makes big tracks around here.'

'I've met him. Smart-looking feller. Got the look of a gambler on him. What does Arlen say about him?'

'Polder's gathering a lot of hard cases. Some known criminals among them. You want I should go head-hunting in Polder's direction, Cleve?'

'Not alone. We'll take a stroll around town together when Shemp gets back.' Stafford led the way back to the front office. 'We'll have the window fixed tomorrow. But not before we teach the hard cases around here some manners.'

Riley's booming laugh echoed in the office, but the sound of gunshots somewhere in town cut off the sound, and as quick as Stafford was in reacting to the disturbance, Riley was faster. The big man jerked open the street door and went out in a hurry, his gun already clutched in his massive left hand.

Stafford followed closely as more shots hammered through the darkness, sending raucous echoes across the town. He compressed his lips, aware that this was the way it was going to be until the law was accepted by the wrongdoers gathered in Concho.

# FOUR

Echoes of the shots were still growling in the distance when Stafford saw Shemp Peck crouching by the hitch-rail outside the hotel where the horses were tethered. The diminutive deputy had drawn both his pistols and was peering around into the shadows, ready for action. Riley pounded forward like a runaway horse, scattering curious townsfolk who were emerging from the saloons to check on the shooting. Stafford took to the street and went forward quickly, gun in hand, passing Riley to reach Peck.

'What gives, Shemp?' Stafford demanded.

'A couple of guns opened up on me the minute I stopped by the horses,' Peck growled. 'They fired from that alley across the street. Nicked the top of my left ear with their first shot.' He chuckled harshly. 'I figure they reckoned I was taller than I am, and if I had been they might have caught me dead centre. Looks like it pays to be short in a job like this, huh?'

'Did you score a hit?' Riley demanded, leaning on the hitch-rail and breathing heavily.

'Of course I did!' Peck sounded indignant. 'Two guns started on me, and when I sent a coupla slugs across the street, one of them packed in immediately. The other was still figuring I'm six feet tall. It's too dark to see, but I reckon my hat must be full of the holes meant for my chest.'

'Cover me and I'll check across the street,' Stafford rapped.

'No need to.' Peck snickered mirthlessly. 'The guy ran along the opposite boardwalk until he was clear, then crossed the street to enter the saloon along there.'

'Let's go get him!' Riley had recovered his breath, and started forward immediately.

Stafford stayed on the street and Peck accompanied him. They were silent until they reached the batwings of the saloon. Riley paused at one side of the entrance and peered into the building. He shook his head and eased back, then looked at Peck as the little deputy stepped on to the sidewalk.

'Did you get a look at him, Shemp?' he bellowed.

'I did better'n that.' Peck grinned. 'I creased him with a slug. That's why he took off. When he entered here he was almost on his knees.'

Stafford pushed through the batwings and paused on the threshold inside the saloon. Riley and Peck joined him, and they stood shoulder to shoulder, looking around the crowded interior. A man was lying on the floor in the centre of the room with a number of men crowding around him, one of them being Griff Polder.

'That guy on the floor is the one I winged,' Peck observed. 'Looks like I hit him harder than I figured.'

'Watch our backs, Riley,' Stafford said, and Peck sided him as he went forward. Men gave way reluctantly. The encompassing silence was heavy, fraught with unspoken hostility which Stafford sensed.

Polder stepped back when he saw Stafford. The suave saloonman had a serious expression on his smooth face.

'He ran in here like a scalded cat,' Polder said. 'I heard shooting out there. Was he concerned with it?'

Peck dropped to one knee beside the man and checked him over. He straightened again almost immediately, shaking his head when he met Stafford's gaze.

'He's gone to greener pastures,' Peck grated. 'I'm sorry, Cleve. We could have questioned him some. There wasn't time to pick my spot on him. But why did he run halfway along the street to this place when he was on his last legs? Do you figure he was coming to report to someone?'

'Does anyone know him?' Stafford asked loudly, and the watching townsmen shuffled their feet and muttered. 'Well?' he persisted. 'Someone must have seen him before the shooting.'

'He was in here with another man, but I hadn't seen either of them before tonight,' Polder volunteered. 'They must have ridden into town today.'

'Go through his pockets, Shemp,' Stafford directed, and the little deputy searched the dead man with a slickness that had been well practised, producing little of interest except a wad of paper money.

'He was well heeled, for a drifter,' Polder observed. 'Do you figure someone paid him to shoot at the law? Dave Pickett tried to gun you, and had a twenty-dollar coin in his possession.'

'I'm not forgetting that,' Stafford spoke grimly. He saw Ben Tudman seated at a table in the background in the company of two range-clad men who looked like hard cases. The Big T rancher was talking seriously, apparently uninterested in what was happening around him. 'Let's go check on that other guy,' he decided. 'Maybe he ain't dead.'

They left the saloon and went back along the street. A crowd was standing by a body lying on the opposite sidewalk. Someone had produced a lantern, and yellow light glared into their eyes as they approached.

'He's dead,' someone said as they arrived. 'Hit plumb centre.'

'Does anyone know him?' Stafford asked.

'I don't know his name, but I've seen him around with some of the Big T outfit,' an informant volunteered.

'Let's go talk with Ben Tudman.' Stafford turned back to the saloon.

'Who's Tudman?' Riley asked.

Stafford explained, and gave an account of his brush with the three Big T riders. They entered the saloon to find Frank Willard, the undertaker, in the process of removing the body.

Tudman was still intent on talking to the two range-clad men seated with him, and Stafford paused by their table. Tudman looked up, a tight grin coming to his lips. He seemed to be singularly unaffected by the shooting that had occurred.

'You're making a good start with your law dealing,' Tudman remarked. 'Mebbe you will make a difference around here.'

'There's a man dead on the sidewalk who was seen around in the company of some of your crew,' Stafford replied. 'Come along and see if you can identify him. If he is one of your men then you've got a lot of explaining to do, Tudman.'

Tudman shook his head. He jerked a thumb at the big man sitting on his left. 'This is Abe Strother,' he introduced. 'My ranch foreman. Abe, go take a look at the galoot in question and see if you know him. But hurry back here. We got a lot to do in the morning, and I wanta be ready for anything.'

Strother got to his feet and headed for the batwings, a big man with a forbidding appearance. He was not tall, but built like the side of a barn. He had massive shoulders and his face showed evidence of past encounters with many fists. His pale eyes were practically hidden under permanently swollen eyebrows, and his cheekbones were puffy, marked by small scars.

'Go with him, Riley,' Stafford said. 'I'll be here talking with Tudman.'

Riley departed and Stafford sat down. Peck stood nearby, looking around the saloon, a scowl on his face.

'I'm gonna start fighting the rustlers,' Tudman said fiercely. 'I've taken more than enough of their shenanigans. I've decided to give Chuck Martin a chance to prove his innocence of rustling by taking him in with me. If he is lily-handed then he'll do his best to fight the stealing. But I can't help thinking he's mixed up in it somehow.'

'It would be better if you held fire until I'm able to ride out and do some checking myself,' Stafford said firmly. 'I'll have this town in hand in a few days.'

'I've waited too long as it is.' Tudman shook his head. 'The uncertainty about who is responsible for the rustling is getting too much to shoulder. At the present rate of losses, I'll be wiped clean in another couple of weeks. I got to do something now.'

'I sympathize with you, but you better be sure of your actions or you could wind up on the wrong side of the law. I'd hate to have to come after you.' Stafford shrugged. 'Don't go off half cocked, Tudman.'

'I got some ideas on who might be back of it all,' the Big T rancher said heavily.

'Share the information with me,' Stafford said. 'I'll need help to put an end to the stealing on the range.'

'It ain't more than suspicion, and I'd be a fool to say anything that might forewarn the thieves that I've cottoned on to their game.' Tudman shook his head. 'I'm making a start in the morning, and when you get done around here you can ride out to my place and pick up what's left of the rustlers. It's too late for me to back down now. I got to go ahead.'

Stafford realized that he would not get Tudman to talk of his suspicions and got to his feet, reluctant to waste more time. Shemp Peck was standing nearby, watching the occupants of the big room, covering Stafford's back, and the big deputy caught the little man's eye and he nodded towards the door. Peck grinned and moved away instantly, and Riley appeared at the batwings as they reached the swing doors. Riley was grinning, massaging the knuckles of his massive right fist.

'That guy Strother is real obnoxious,' he declared. 'Didn't wanta co-operate, and started bad-mouthing the law when I told him I didn't believe he didn't know that dead guy. Heck he didn't even get a look at the dead man before denying that he knew him. When he started waving his arms around I figured he was fixing to crack me on the jaw so I downed him.'

'Where is he now?' Stafford demanded.

'Having a quiet sleep on the sidewalk beside the dead man. I figure to throw him in a cell for tonight. Did I do right, Cleve?'

'Sure thing.' Stafford smiled. He walked out to the sidewalk and his two sidekicks followed closely. 'Shemp, did you hear what Ben Tudman was saying when I was at his table?'

'Yeah. He's gonna take the law into his own hands and do us out of a job.'

'That's right.' Stafford nodded. 'And that's all right so long as he tangles with the rustlers and not some innocent rancher. He figures to ride out at dawn, and I want you to trail him, watch him to see what he does. I need to know what he's up to. I don't trust him any more than I trust the rest of the men around here. He says he's planning on riding with Chuck Martin and the M Bar outfit to fight the rustlers. Keep an eye on their movements until you find out what they get up to.'

'Leave it to me,' Peck nodded. 'But I sure hate the thought of missing some of the fun around here. Can't we leave the rustling until after the town has been quietened?'

'You'll get more than your share of fun on the range, or I miss my guess,' Stafford said grimly. 'Do you know if Bill Harra is in town yet?'

'He left us about ten miles outside of town. Said he wanted to get in ahead of us,' Riley's voice boomed. 'He'll be nosing around somewhere. He's got a talent for digging out details, and he'll come out of the woodwork the minute he's got something to report.'

'I would have preferred to have him around us.' Stafford frowned as he considered. 'I'll give him a couple of days on his own. If he can't pick up something in that time then he'll be wasting his time. You get off now, Shemp, and don't take any chances out there on the range.'

'You know me, Cleve!' The little man chuckled and moved away into the shadows, fading quickly into oblivion. His spurs sounded momentarily on the sidewalk, then silence settled.

'And what are we gonna do?' Riley asked. 'I'll go put that Strother guy in a cell. He'll be back to his senses now.'

'Let's attend to him,' Stafford agreed, and they went along the street to where a small group of men were still standing on the sidewalk around two inert figures.

Frank Willard, the undertaker, was pushing a handcart along the street just ahead of them, and he paused when they reached him. He leaned on the cart as he regarded them, his thin face expressionless.

'I'm finding it a mite hard to keep up with you,' he said mildly. 'My place is filled to overflowing with customers awaiting burial. If you keep on like this I shan't be able to cope.'

'I think we've about finished for tonight,' Stafford told him. 'But I reckon tomorrow is gonna be hectic if I know anything at all about law dealing.'

Abe Strother, the Big T ramrod, was stirring on the sidewalk. Riley grasped the man by his shirt front and lifted him bodily, shaking him like a dog with a rat. Strother opened his eyes and began to struggle, but was helpless in Riley's grasp.

'Don't make the mistake of resisting,' Riley advised. 'If I have to put you asleep again you won't wake up in time for breakfast. You're gonna be our first guest in the cells, so come along quietly.'

'You can't lock me up!' Strother protested. 'I ain't

done nothing wrong. What kind of law do you run? I didn't do anything.'

'It's your word against mine.' Riley was implacable. 'And if you don't know whose word they will believe then you've got a lot to learn.'

'I've got some work to do tonight,' Strother protested. 'Big T is moving against the rustlers in the morning. We're going out to do your work for you and you're slapping me in jail! Heck, you ain't got enough friends around here to handle me like this!'

'Mebbe you're right.' Stafford smiled grimly. 'All right, you can go. I'll talk to you again later. And when you see your outfit again you tell them that as from tomorrow the town is off limits to men carrying guns.'

'You ain't never gonna make that stick,' Strother rasped. 'Where's my hogleg?' he demanded, slapping his holster and finding it empty. 'I'm gonna need that.'

Riley took the man's gun from his waistband and thrust it deep into Strother's holster. 'You better get out of here now,' he bellowed. 'I don't like your face, Mister. If you try anything else with me I'll rearrange your features so your own mother won't recognize you.'

Strother departed quickly, and Stafford watched him until the man had disappeared into the shadows.

'You don't like him,' Stafford observed. 'What's biting you, Howie?'

'I got the feeling that he's against us,' Riley spoke

thoughtfully. 'I can't put my finger on it at the moment, but he'll bear watching. I'm never far wrong when I get this kind of feeling.'

'Shemp will be watching him.' Stafford stifled a yawn. 'I don't reckon there's anything else we can do tonight so we might as well call it a day and rest up for tomorrow, which looks like being a big day. 'We'll hit the sack in the jail, Howie. We got to stick together like a burr and a blanket until we get the town settled down.

'Suits me.' Riley shrugged his big shoulders. 'I don't care what happens so long as I get a chance at Strother before this finishes. I sure don't like that guy.'

'I respect your hunches.' Stafford grinned as they walked towards the law office, which was shrouded in shadow. He paused and dropped a hand to his holstered gun as a figure moved slightly in the darkness ahead, and a low-toned voice called a quick warning.

'Hold it, Cleve. This is Harra. I got something for you, but let's make it quick. I got a lot to do tonight.'

Stafford went forward, relieved that Bill Harra had come to contact him so quickly. The deputy was accustomed to working undercover, and generally went straight to the heart of any crookedness he was investigating. They went into the law office, and Stafford lit a lamp. Harra pulled back into a corner, turning his back to the big, broken front window.

'You seem nervous,' Stafford observed.

'I don't need to be seen around you,' Harra said.

'I'm due to ride out with a couple of rustlers some time before dawn.'

'Tell me more.' Stafford eyed the tall, thin deputy. 'It hasn't taken you long to make contact with the other side.'

'The minute I walked into Polder's saloon a guy named Mart Crayle pounced on me as if I had a notice tied round my neck. He was mixed up in that rustling job we nosed into over by Mulejaw Bend last year and took a slug before the showdown. He didn't get to hear that I was responsible for the gang's downfall. He remembered me as a good rustler and has promised me a job with the local cattle stealers. I'm gonna string along with him, and I'll be in touch with you soon as I get the lowdown on the bunch.'

'Shemp is gonna trail some men we suspect of being mixed up with the rustling,' Stafford said. 'Keep an eye open for him out on the range, and watch your step, Bill.'

Harra nodded. His manner was quiet, his angular face in repose. But his blue eyes were filled with a brightness that indicated his pleasure at being involved in the dangerous business he had chosen for a career. He was dressed in sober range clothes and wore a cartridge belt low on his right hip. His holster, containing a .44 Remington, was tied down on his thigh. He had the appearance of a long rider down on his luck.

'I'd better be on my way,' he said, turning to the door. 'I'll get word to you soon as I know who my rustling friends are. Watch your back, Cleve. I ain't been in town long but I sure heard a lot about what is likely to happen to you in the next twenty-four hours.

'Sure.' Stafford smiled. 'I expect to have the town tamed in a couple of days. Then we'll move out to the range.'

Harra grinned and departed silently. Stafford looked at Riley, and the big man grimaced, his face unusually serious.

'I don't like the way we've split into two pairs.' Riley voiced the doubts that Stafford was feeling. 'It's gonna need more than two of us in town tomorrow.'

'We'll get some local help,' Stafford replied. 'First thing in the morning I'll see about getting a town marshal appointed, and it'll be his job to disarm anyone inside of town limits.'

'And he'll need an army at his back to make that law stick,' Riley persisted.

'You think we're going in half-cocked, Howie?'

Riley shrugged. 'It ain't to my liking. That's all I got to say. I reckon we need the four of us together to face down the town. We've heard a lot about how tough the crooks are, and they'll come at us bull-headed soon as we show our faces on the street tomorrow. I'd feel happier if we was all together.'

'We'll handle it,' Stafford said. 'Don't worry about it. I'm not about to take any wild chances. And I figure we're gonna have to be on guard through the night so you'd better get your head down first. I'll be on duty until two in the morning, when I'll give you a call to take over until dawn.'

'Suits me. I'll bed down in one of the cells. But first I got to take care of my horse. I'll be about fifteen minutes.'

'I'll be here when you get back,' Stafford told him, and Riley departed.

Stafford found a broom and swept the office clear of broken glass. He was sitting at the desk checking through the record books when the door was opened and Pete Boxall, the town mayor, came into the office accompanied by a small man dressed in a black broadcloth suit, and looking every inch a gambler with his sombre appearance.

'Stafford, I got a town marshal here. This is Walt Sand. He's been a town lawman around the county for a number of years.'

'Yeah, I've seen him around.' Stafford got to his feet. 'Howdy, Sand. You've made yourself quite a reputation handling town law.'

'Don't believe all you hear,' Sand replied. He had a deep voice for a man of his size. 'But I've never failed in any job I took on, and I reckon Concho is one tough town. I'll have a couple of deputies in here some time tomorrow, and we'll take care of the town. Do you reckon you can make your "no guns" law work?'

'Do you think *you* can make it work?' Stafford countered. 'You'll be the one with the job of enforcing it.'

'Sure. If that's what you want then that's what

you'll get.' Sand glanced around the office. 'I'll work from here, huh? Looks like you've already been troubled by the other side, but we'll soon lick this place into shape.'

'The flies have been biting some,' Stafford replied. 'There'll be a new window put in tomorrow, and then we'll be ready for business as usual. I'm glad you're able to come in on our side, Sand. Do you wanta sack down in the jail?'

'Sure thing. This is where the action is gonna be, you can bet. I wouldn't miss this showdown for a year's pay.'

Pete Boxall grinned, evidently relieved with the way the new marshal was accepting the situation. 'I've been asking around town,' he said, 'and there are a number of honest men who will take up guns with you if you should need extra help. You'll have to let me know.'

'There's nothing we can do until tomorrow,' Stafford said. 'Then we'll know which way the wind blows. Thanks for your help, Mr Mayor.'

Boxall departed, anxious to be on his way, and Stafford showed Sand into the cell block. The little town marshal shook his head as he noted the squalor.

'I heard a lot about the way Boone Hickey was running the law around here,' he said. 'Pity he's gone. I was looking forward to seeing him through gunsmoke. Didn't you have an order to arrest him?'

Stafford shook his head. 'Nope. He was told to ride

back to Whiskey River to Sheriff Arlen, and left town fast.'

Sand grinned and opened his mouth to reply, but his voice was drowned out by a fusillade of shots that sent heavy echoes blasting through the town. Stafford reacted quickly, but Sand proved that he was quick-witted. He reached the street door one step ahead of Stafford and they darted outside. But by the time they reached the sidewalk the shooting had ceased, and they looked around into the darkness as gun echoes growled and faded away. . . .

# FIVE

Stafford crouched in the shadows, gun drawn and cocked ready for action. The new town marshal was by his side, holding his gun, and they listened to the dying echoes of the shooting, trying to deduce the direction of the disturbance.

'I've got a deputy who went along to the stable to take care of his horse,' Stafford said. 'Could be he found trouble. I'd better get along the street fast. Do you wanta come or stay here?'

'If there is trouble then I'll need to be with you,' Sand replied. 'Let's go.'

They ran along the street, ignoring the curious townsmen who were appearing on the sidewalk. Stafford was aware that Riley could take care of himself, but the odds were against them, and he was worried that his big sidekick had been overwhelmed by the opposition.

The livery barn was in darkness when Stafford reached it. He paused in cover and surveyed the big doorway. Silence had closed in and nothing moved.

The night breeze was steady, and the sound of a horse kicking in its stall sounded unnaturally loud.

'Howie, can you hear me?' Stafford called, gun lifted and ready for action. His eyes were narrowed in an attempt to pierce the shadows.

'Yeah, I'm in the barn, Cleve,' came the instant reply. 'I walked into a gun trap, but I figure they pulled out soon as I started shooting. They left by the back door, but I've got the feeling they are still laying for me. I'm coming out now. Cover me, huh?'

'You're covered,' Stafford replied grimly. He sensed the new town marshal's presence nearby but could not see the man in the darkness. He watched the blackness of the open doorway of the barn, and saw a movement in the shadows as Riley emerged.

The next instant a gun exploded in the dense shadows surrounding the left-hand front corner of the wooden building. A long plume of reddish flame speared towards Riley, who went down into the dust. Stafford replied to the shot without thinking about it, his reflexes hair-triggered. He sent three spaced shots at the gun flash, and heavy echoes fled through the night. An uneasy silence followed as the echoes faded.

'I reckon you got him,' Riley called. 'He bored my hat and parted my hair for me, but I ain't hurt. I'm ready to try again.'

'Come ahead,' Stafford replied, cocking his gun. 'You're still covered.'

Riley arose once more and backed away from the entrance of the stable. This time nothing happened, and he reached Stafford's side without further incident.

'That was too close for comfort,' Riley said casually. 'I walked into cross-fire soon as I entered the barn. They figured someone would bring the horse in before long. I should have thought of that. I reckon I must be getting careless in my old age, huh?'

'Let's check out that left corner,' Stafford said. 'I reckon I hit the gun that fired from there.'

'Cover me,' Riley said tensely. 'It's my job.' He stepped out into the open and went forward resolutely, and Walt Sand eased forward and went with him.

Stafford moved to the left to keep the corner under his gun. Riley uttered an imprecation when he reached the barn.

'There's a body lying here,' he reported. 'We'll need a light to see who it is.'

'Get one out of the barn,' Stafford replied.

Riley moved off and entered the barn, to reappear moments later carrying a lighted lantern that threw a yellow glare into the surrounding darkness. Stafford averted his gaze and watched the encompassing shadows. He guessed that the ambushers had departed now, and moved out of cover and walked to the corner of the barn. Riley reached the spot first and held the lantern aloft to light up the area. Sand was crouching by the corner, facing the darkness, his gun poised for action.

Stafford gazed at the dead man sprawled by the

corner. A discarded pistol lay some inches from a nerveless, outflung hand. There were two blood-stains on the dead man's shirt front, and Riley chuckled as he bent to inspect them, pulling the fabric of the shirt tight to see exactly where the slugs had struck.

'That was mighty good shooting in the dark, Cleve,' he observed. 'I wonder who the galoot is?'

Stafford could hear men gathering just out of range of the lantern light, and glanced over his shoulder.

'One of you can come forward,' he called. 'We got a dead man here and need a name for him.'

A figure materialized out of the night, and Doc Wilson came to Stafford's side. He looked at the still, upturned face of the dead man.

'That's Jake Pilling, the stableman,' he said instantly. Him and Al Jory run the place for Griff Polder.'

'What in hell was he doing out here with a gun?' Riley demanded. 'He near killed me.' He removed his hat and rubbed his fingers through his hair. 'Bored my hat and near took a length of scalp from my head. He sure was acting unfriendly.'

'Griff Polder owns the stable,' Wilson volunteered. 'Mebbe Pilling was acting on Polder's orders.'

'Polder again,' Stafford mused. 'His name is crop-ping up too often for it to be a coincidence. I figure we better have a talk with Polder. Howie, this is Walt Sand, the new town marshal. Sand, this is Howard Riley, one of my special deputies.'

'I know the name,' Riley said. 'Walt Sand. Yeah, you been working for the law in a number of places around the county. Had a lot of success, too. Heard how you smashed the Yarrup gang a couple of years ago. How come you've taken over here?'

'My last place got too quiet,' Sand replied. 'I heard things were jumping around here so I decided to take a hand.'

'Let's get ourselves a drink,' Stafford suggested. 'In Polder's saloon.'

They left the stable and went back along the street. A number of men were on the sidewalks, seeking information about the latest disturbance. Stafford saw Griff Polder standing on the boardwalk in front of his bar, and the well-dressed saloonman backed into the building as Stafford crowded forward.

'What was that shooting about?' Polder's dark eyes were glittering as he acknowledged the deadly intent in Stafford's manner.

'Riley walked into a gun trap when he took his horse into the livery barn,' Stafford replied. 'He was shot at from cover, and I nailed the backshooter, who turned out to be Jake Pilling, one of your stablemen. Pilling is dead. You own the livery, Polder, and I'm wondering if Pilling was acting on your orders.'

'Why should I know anything about it?' Polder demanded angrily.

Riley reached out a big hand and secured a hold on Polder's shirt front. He exerted his strength and the saloonman's feet almost left the floor. He was dragged up on to his toes under the power of Riley's surging strength.

'Come clean with us.' Riley spoke grimly. 'Pilling damn near put a slug through my head. I wanta know what he was doing outside the barn, using a gun against me. He was waiting for me, and some-one gave him orders.'

'I want to know why a number of the men in your employ are taking up arms against the law,' Stafford said. 'Dave Pickett was your man. It looks like he was acting on your orders, Polder. What have you got to say about that?'

'I don't know what it's all about.' Polder was struggling ineffectually against Riley's grip. 'And you can't treat me like this. I own about half this town and my taxes help keep you in a job.'

'I'm gonna do my job to the letter,' Stafford decided. 'Take him to the jail and throw him in a cell, Howie. We'll see if a night behind bars will make him change his tune.'

'I'll handle it,' Sand said. 'I'm the town marshal and I'll take care of the details. Are you carrying a gun, Polder?'

'No. I don't make a habit of being armed.'

Riley checked Polder with a practised hand and nodded.

'He's clean.'

Stafford looked around the saloon as Sand departed with Polder, and noted that Ben Tudman and his men were no longer present. He wondered about the Big T rancher, and hoped he had done the right thing by sending Shemp Peck out to tail the cowman. Crossing to the bar, he ordered beer for himself and Riley, and discovered that he could not relax. There were too many questions confronting him, and at the moment he was getting no answers.

Doc Wilson came into the saloon and made for Stafford. The doctor looked as if he had something on his mind, and Stafford signalled to the barkeep.

'Give the doc whatever he wants,' he said.

'Whiskey.' Wilson looked at Stafford, his eyes filled with uncertainty. 'I think you've made a mistake by throwing Polder in jail,' he said.

'Tell me about it,' Stafford invited.

'I got an idea that Polder is behind much of the local crime, but you won't prove it by jailing him. In my job I have to be out at all hours, day and night. I see things that most other folks miss, and for some time I've suspected that Polder is running the crookedness. But I wasn't able to pass on my suspicions to Boone Hickey because that deputy sure acted as if he was in cahoots with Polder, so I contacted Sheriff Arlen with my suspicions.'

'So that's why the sheriff sent me in here!' Stafford nodded. 'He seemed to know a lot about conditions here. What's on your mind, Doc? Finger those responsible for the trouble around here and we'll put an end to their doings.'

'Like I said, I'm certain Polder is your man. He started out by taking over some of the smaller businesses in town – the livery barn and the lumber mill. His strong-arm bullies forced the owners to sell. I heard all about it, and treated a couple of men who had been beaten up by Polder's thugs. I talked to the mayor but he couldn't talk to Hickey about it because the deputy looked like he was in Polder's pocket. Our hands have been tied until you arrived.'

'That's fine,' Stafford nodded. 'I reckon the sheriff will arrest Hickey the minute he shows up in Whiskey River. I've got Polder behind bars now, and tomorrow we'll start collecting evidence aainst him. Who else around here is crooked?'

'There are a number of hard men who put their muscle behind Polder.' Wilson glanced towards a card table that was crowded with players. 'That's Grover Sheldon in that fancy jacket. He runs the gambling in here. He's killed three men at that table in the past month, and I know for a fact that Polder has taken over two small cow spreads recently from ranchers who couldn't pay their gambling debts. I talked to the womenfolk who were left to fend for themselves after their men were killed.'

Stafford's eyes narrowed as he listened, then he nodded. 'Howie, ' he said. 'The gambler wearing the fancy jacket at that table over there is crooked. Go watch him, and arrest him if you see any underhand play.'

'Sure thing.' Riley moved away from the bar and took up a position by the table in question.

'You better watch the man with the shotgun sitting on that chair at the top of the stairs,' Wilson warned.

Stafford had already marked the position of the

shotgun guard. He eased his pistol in its holster and moved along the bar until he was satisfied that he was covering the situation.

'The man in the red shirt at the table is Ira Benson,' Wilson said in an undertone to Stafford. 'He owns the B Bar B ranch, and, judging by his expression, it looks like Sheldon has got him by the short hairs.'

Stafford could not see the rancher's play, but he was aware of the tension growing around the table. He saw Riley ease his gun in its holster, and readied himself for action.

'I don't know much about playing cards,' Riley said suddenly, his booming voice freezing the action around the table. 'But I do know it ain't right for cards to be dealt from the bottom of the pack.'

His words triggered off immediate action around the table. Sheldon pulled a gun out of a shoulder holster. Riley unlimbered his pistol, and Stafford, seeing the shotgun guard raising his weapon to cover the table, drew his six-gun and fired at the man, who crumpled instantly, discharging his fearsome weapon into the ceiling as Stafford's bullet drilled through his heart.

Riley was the first to fire around the table, and Sheldon dropped his hideout gun to slump forward across the green baize, spilling blood over the cards. The quick blasts of the shooting shook the saloon, and men froze as the harsh echoes faded. Stafford saw some tough-looking men sitting at the table, took them for Polder's men, and called urgently.

'Don't anybody reach for a gun. The law is taking

over in here. Cool it and nobody else will get hurt.'
He paced forward to stand beside the watchful Riley,
and shocked faces were turned towards them.
'Benson, don't you know better than to play in a
crooked game?' he continued, and saw the rancher
flinch. 'You must know that you're not the first
rancher to lose out at this table in this saloon.'

'Yeah.' Benson grimaced. 'I was losing all right,
and there wasn't nothing I could do about it with
Polder's gunnies sitting in on the game. Until you
showed up, that is. But I wasn't in this alone. There's
half a dozen men around the saloon who were ready
to step in and back my play if things got tough.
We've had enough of Polder's trickery. I'm gathering
proof of what's been going on in here, and planned to
report it to the sheriff.'

'Fine. But I'm here now and I'll handle this. Any
proof of bad play that you have, you can tell me and
we'll sort it out.' Stafford looked around at the faces
at the table. Doc Wilson had moved around to where
Sheldon was lying face-down and was examining
the gambler.

'He's still alive,' he reported. 'But I'll have to do a
lot of work on him before you'll be able to talk to
him. I'd like to get him over to my surgery.'

'Go ahead,' Stafford nodded. 'Get men you can
trust to take Sheldon to your place and I'll check
with you later. Benson, you stick with me. We'll talk
when I get time. Which of these men at the table do
you suspect of working in cahoots with Polder? Tell
me and I'll arrest them.'

'Poggin there, in the green shirt, is one of Polder's top guns,' Benson said without hesitation.

'You watch what you're saying.' Poggin pushed back his chair and surged to his feet. 'No one calls me crooked and lives.'

Riley leaned sideways towards the gunman and slammed the long barrel of his pistol against the man's head. Poggin let out a yell and went sprawling to the floor, shaking his head. His hat saved him from serious damage, and he twisted like a cat and reached for the gun holstered on his right hip. Riley squeezed off a shot that put a red splotch on Poggin's shirt in the region of his right shoulder and the gunman immediately lost interest in the proceedings.

'Anyone else?' Stafford demanded as the echoes of the shot faded away.

'Al Gauvin, next to Poggin, always backs Poggin's play,' Benson said. 'We think Gauvin and Poggin killed Pete Johnson and Mike Talbot, who lost their ranches to Polder. And you won't have to look past Polder to stop the rustling.'

'That's interesting.' Stafford motioned with his pistol. 'Let's get this place cleared out. Doc, you take care of the injured men. Howie, take Gauvin to jail and put him behind bars. Then go along to the Doc's and bring in Poggin when he's been treated.' He raised his voice and shouted at the patrons. 'Come on. Everybody move out. This place is closed as of now. Empty the place, and fast.'

The barkeep began to protest vociferously and Stafford glanced at Riley.

'Take the barkeep with you and lock him up with Gauvin.'

Riley grinned and ushered Gauvin and the barkeep, still protesting, to the batwings, where he made them stand against the wall by the entrance. A stream of men moved in the same direction, and moments later the bar was deserted, except for the wounded men and those who had remained to help the doctor. Benson, the rancher, remained at Stafford's side.

'Have you got a problem, Howie?' Stafford called to his deputy.

'Nary a one. I'm waiting for you to clear out so the barkeep can lock up. Then I'll lock him up.'

'You sure know how to handle the law,' Doc Wilson said. 'I never thought I'd see the day Griff Polder was bested in his own saloon.'

'We haven't started cleaning up yet.' Stafford grinned. 'Just wait until tomorrow.'

The doctor organized his helpers to carry out the wounded men. Stafford stood outside on the sidewalk while the place was closed, then accompanied Riley to the jail, their prisoners walking ahead of them. Benson followed behind, and Stafford glanced at the rancher.

'So you were testing Polder's set-up,' he said. 'That was a mighty dangerous thing to do.'

'That's right. But I knew I was next on Polder's list. After what happened to some in our community we realized it was only a matter of time before the rest of us were attacked. We complained to

Boone Hickey, but he wouldn't do a blame thing.'

'So what was Polder's play?'

'He made low offers for our spreads, and when we refused he started using strong-arm tactics to get us unsettled. Most of us had taken out loans with the bank, and Polder seems to have some kind of a hold over Hoffmeyer, the banker. Leastways, Hoffmeyer began to badger us for extra interest on Polder's say-so. He began calling in our notes, knowing we couldn't pay.'

'So you played deeper into his hands by gambling in his saloon in the hope of getting back some of your cash, huh?' Stafford shook his head. 'That sure sounds like fool play!'

'We were desperate,' Benson said angrily. 'We got no help from the law. Hickey was working in cahoots with Polder.'

'You got evidence of that?'

'We've got plenty of evidence, if you can prove that we'll be safe after we give it.'

'You saw the way we handle the law,' Stafford said. 'It's always like that with us. Give me proof of Polder's guilt and he won't ever walk out of the jail a free man.'

'He's got hard cases out on the spreads he stole,' Benson said tensely. 'They're helping with the rustling. I've seen some of them at work.'

'We'll deal with them in good time. Look, I'm gonna be real busy until morning, so why don't you get together with your friends and sort out the evidence I'll need to nail Polder? Come and see me first thing in the morning, huh?'

'Sure thing.' Benson smiled. 'This is more like it.' He turned and departed along the sidewalk.

Stafford followed Riley into the law office. Riley took his prisoners into the cell block. Walt Sand was sitting at the desk, grinning in satisfaction. He looked up to meet Stafford's gaze.

'This is the way law dealing should be done,' he said. 'I put Polder in a cell. He's asked to see his lawyer, one Alford Ward.'

'He's entitled to see a lawyer,' Stafford nodded. 'Locate Ward and bring him in.'

Sand departed, and Riley emerged from the cell block, rattling the big bunch of keys. He seemed to be in high spirits.

'Say, Cleve, we've made a good start around here, huh?' he demanded. 'Shemp and Bill are missing all the fun, and that's a fact. Is there anything else you want me to do tonight? If not I'll hit the sack.'

'You go ahead, Howie. Like I said earlier, I'll stand first watch. I'll call you about two in the morning. But don't count too much on getting some sleep.'

Riley nodded and returned to the cell block. Stafford sat down at the desk and began to write out his report of the incidents that had taken place since his arrival. Silence closed in around the jail and there was peace for the first time since he had come into town.

Minutes later, when he was nearing the end of his report, he heard the sound of feet on the sidewalk outside, and threw down his pen and dropped a hand to the butt of his holstered gun. The boots stopped outside the office door and silence ensued. Getting to his feet, Stafford moved away from the desk, covering the street door. With no glass in the front window, he felt more vulnerable than usual.

There was a scratching sound outside the door and Stafford cocked his gun and prepared for action. He leaned across the desk and snuffed out the lamp, narrowing his eyes against the darkness that swooped into the office. A lantern was hanging nearby on an awning post outside, and dim light filtered in through the window.

Stafford waited stolidly, gun poised in his hand. The footsteps he heard had halted outside the door and had not gone on, so someone was standing out there in the night. He moved to the door, careful to keep to one side in case shots were fired through the woodwork. He could feel a cold breeze coming in at the paneless window, which was making his eyes water, and he ducked below the level of the window and moved to its far corner, raising up carefully to peer outside. He could see at an angle across the outside of the doorway, but nothing was visible beyond the window.

The lantern hanging on the awning post outside was suddenly moved. Stafford could not see it, but shadows danced across the doorway, and he sneaked back into the far corner of the office.

The next instant the lantern was hurled into the office. Stafford saw the hand that was clutching it, and ducked as the lantern narrowly missed him and crashed upon the bare boards. The glass smashed, and flame seared the woodwork, spreading quickly as the contents of the lantern ran in all directions.

Stafford wasted no more time. He dived for the street door, and as he jerked it open he heard the sound of running footsteps fading quickly into the night.

# SIX

Stafford threw himself flat on the sidewalk and peered to the right when his ears picked up the sound of someone running away in that direction. He saw a figure moving quickly some ten yards away and lifted his gun. His eyes were narrowed as he considered the situation. He drew a bead on the retreating figure, which was outlined against the light of a lantern further along the street.

'Hold it right there,' he yelled. 'I got you covered. Stop and put your hands up.'

The man glanced back over his shoulder without pausing, and, when Stafford accepted that the fugitive was not going to stop, he fired a single shot. The gun crashed and the man pitched forward to fall heavily on the boardwalk. His right foot twitched several times before he slumped inertly.

Stafford turned quickly and went back into the office. Holstering his gun, he grabbed a pail of water that was standing on a chair near the door leading into the cell block. The fire was taking hold rapidly, and he swilled the water over it, partially dousing the flames. He was stamping on the still-burning boards when the door to the cell block was thrust open and Riley appeared from within, gun in hand.

'I heard a shot,' the big man bellowed. 'More trouble?'

'Stamp out these flames,' Stafford directed. 'I got someone down on the sidewalk.'

He ran outside and hurried along the sidewalk, drawing his pistol as he neared the unmoving figure. There was a lantern burning just ahead, hanging from a post, and he could see that the man's hands were outflung and empty. He slowed and approached carefully. A sigh gusted from him when he tugged at a heavy shoulder, rolled the man on to his back, and found himself looking into the fleshy face of Boone Hickey, the deputy he had come into Concho to relieve of duty.

Hickey was dead. Stafford's bullet had struck him dead centre between the shoulder blades. Stafford straightened as Riley approached, and the big man cursed when he recognized Hickey.

'Did that skunk throw the lantern in the window, Cleve?'

'He was running away when I got outside,' Stafford replied, 'and didn't stop when I challenged him.'

Riley grimaced. 'The sheriff said he had some bad reports about Hickey. I guess this confirms them, huh?'

'It looks that way.' Stafford glanced around, and

shook his head when he spotted townsmen coming to check on the latest disturbance. 'We sure got the men of this town on the hop tonight,' he observed. 'If this keeps up, there won't be many left come morning for us to investigate.'

'We'll need to find out who was friendly with Hickey. It was a pity you had to kill him, Cleve. He might have talked, and that would have saved us some time.'

'There was no time to try for a wing shot.' Stafford spoke grimly. He saw the diminutive figure of Walt Sand coming along the sidewalk and narrowed his gaze when he saw a tall thin figure at the marshal's heels. The man was dressed in a store suit, and Stafford immediately pegged him as the lawyer.

'What happened?' Sand demanded when he arrived, and cursed soundly when Stafford told him. 'I've heard a lot about Hickey,' Sand continued, 'and all of it was bad. Heck, attempting to burn down the law office ain't something you would expect from a deputy, huh? Mebbe he was feeling the pinch because you came into town and ordered him back to the sheriff.'

'He sure didn't like it when I told him.' Stafford saw the undertaker coming along the sidewalk. He turned his attention to the man accompanying Sand. 'You're Ward, the lawyer, huh?' he demanded.

'That's right. I understand you've arrested Griff Polder. I'd like to see him.'

'Sure. Come into the office.' Stafford went back along the sidewalk, leaving Sand to deal with the undertaker. Riley accompanied him, and then took Ward into the cell block to see Polder.

Stafford looked around the office. Smoke irritated his nostrils, but the fire was out. He shook his head as he considered what had happened. The evening was past now, and he saw that the hands of the clock on the wall were close to pointing out midnight. He knew it was going to be a long night, and longed for dawn so that he could push forward with his plans to master the wrongdoers in the town.

Riley came back into the office, jangling the cell keys. 'I locked the lawyer in with Polder,' he said. 'He'll have to shout when he wants out. You ain't gonna turn Polder loose on the lawyer's say-so, are you, Cleve?'

'You know me better than that,' Stafford growled. 'Polder will stay where he is until I've checked him out. I got to get statements from Benson and the other small ranchers. They seem to think they've got the deadwood on Polder.'

The street door opened and Doc Wilson came into the office. He gazed at the blackened floorboards. His face was lined with weariness when he looked at Stafford.

'Did Hickey do this?' he asked.

'I got him pegged as the culprit. Did Hickey have any special friends around town?'

'Mostly hard cases.' Wilson shrugged his thin shoulders. 'I figure they'll all leave town when they hear what's happened to Hickey.'

The lawyer called from the cells and Riley went

back to him. Stafford sat down at the desk and tried to relax. Ward emerged from the cell block and came to the desk.

'Polder tells me he hasn't been charged with anything,' the lawyer said. 'Do you have any charges against him?'

Stafford nodded. 'That's why he's behind bars. Come back in the morning and we'll talk it over then. Right now I'm busy. But I expect to charge Polder with murder and rustling when I've got statements from witnesses.'

'Who are the witnesses?' Ward was tall and thin, with alert brown eyes.

'I'm not prepared to mention names at this stage.' Stafford shrugged. 'You'll have to do like I say. I'll talk to you some more in the morning.'

Ward shook his head, opening his mouth as if to persist, but he read the expression on Stafford's face, nodded, then turned and departed. Riley grinned at Stafford.

'I figure he's got an idea that he's the most impor- tant man in town, Cleve. And I guess he's forgotten more about the law than we'll ever know, huh?'

'I know enough to handle this business,' Stafford replied. 'Perhaps you can get some sleep now, huh?'

'What are you gonna do?' Riley stifled a yawn and rasped the fingers of his right hand through the growth of stubble on his large chin. 'If you've got anything to do then I'll go along with you. It's getting a mite late to sleep now. Are there any hard cases we can go after? Hickey must have some pards around town.'

'I plan to make a round of the town now,' Stafford said. 'And I guess you better go along with me.' He looked at the silent Doc Wilson. 'Something on your mind, Doc?' he demanded. 'You're looking as worried as I feel.'

'I came past the Cattleman's Bar a few minutes ago and saw half a dozen hard cases in there. Looked like they was talking up trouble for someone so I thought you better know about it. They are men who spend a lot of time in the saloons, gambling and drinking, but don't seem to have regular jobs. If I were in charge of the law around here I'd stick them all in jail.'

'Thanks for the tip,' Stafford smiled. 'We'll go look them up. Will you come along, Walt?'

'Sure thing,' the new town marshal replied eagerly. 'The more we do tonight the less there will be tomorrow.'

Sand locked the office despite the broken window, and dropped the keys into a pocket. They left the office and walked along the boardwalk accompanied by the doctor, who left them at the batwings of the Cattleman's Bar. Stafford looked into the bar and saw that the place was practically deserted. There was one man standing at the bar talking with the tender, and four men were seated at a table in a far corner, engrossed in a game of poker.

Stafford shouldered his way through the batwings and strode to the bar. The tender moved towards him, wiping the bar with a damp cloth.

'Three beers,' Stafford said, and felt in a vest pocket for a silver coin. 'You're quiet tonight, huh? Where is that bunch of men who were in here a few minutes ago? I heard they were priming themselves for some kinda trouble.'

'They left kind of sudden,' the tender replied. 'Got some business out of town, so I heard them say. I guess they'll be at the livery stable about now.'

'Forget the beer. It'll have to keep.' Stafford turned as a thought struck him, and left the bar in a hurry. Riley and Sand had to stretch their legs to stay with him.

'What's on your mind?' Riley demanded.

'Just a hunch.' Stafford lengthened his stride until he was almost running along the boardwalk towards the stable. Riley stayed with him easily enough, but the diminutive town marshal had to run to stay in touch.

When they reached the livery barn the place was in total darkness. Stafford went close and looked in at the big open front door. There was no light inside, and no movement.

'What's going on?' Riley demanded, disappointment edging his tone. 'They couldn't have left town that fast, unless their mounts were ready saddled in here.'

'I got a feeling they might have something else in mind.' Stafford turned on his heel. 'Let's get back to the jail. If these hard cases are in Polder's pay they might just be planning to spring him loose.'

They hastened back along the street. The town was quiet now, and most of the buildings were in darkness. Stafford paused when they were still some distance from the law office. He peered into the darkness surrounding the building but saw no movement.

'You two go to the front door,' he directed. 'I figure they'll be at the rear if they're anywhere.'

'I'll go with you,' Riley said instantly. 'You always get all the action.'

Stafford did not argue. He turned into an alley on the right while Sand went on along the sidewalk. It was dark in the alley and Stafford had to feel his way along to the back lots. Riley was silent at his back, moving surprisingly quietly for such a big man.

They reached the rear end of the alley, where the darkness was complete. Stafford paused, unable to see, but his keen ears picked up the sound of a horse champing on its bit, and a hoof stamped just ahead, the sound coming from the direction of the jail.

'Sounds like you're right,' Riley hissed eagerly in Stafford's ear. 'Them buzzards are after Polder. Let's go give 'em hell.'

They went forward slowly, a step at a time, and Stafford drew his pistol and cocked the weapon. They had almost reached the jail before his narrowed eyes picked out the outlines of several horses. Pausing, he looked for human figures, and saw the shape of a man at the back door of the jail, standing with the horses and holding their reins.

Moving in silently, Stafford was tensing himself to jump the man when shots rang out from the front of the building. The horse holder cursed, and sensed or heard Stafford's movement as the big chief deputy lunged forward. He turned quickly, but Stafford was upon him before he could draw a gun. Stafford's pistol rose and fell and the man crumpled silently to the ground.

Stafford fired two shots into the air and the half a dozen horses stampeded instantly, galloping away into the darkness of the back lots.

'Watch this man and the rear of the jail,' Stafford rapped as more shooting erupted from the front of the law office. 'Sand sounds like he might be in trouble.'

He ran along the alley beside the jail, heading for the street, making noise now. A gun flashed from the street end of the alley and a bullet crackled past his head. He returned fire and kept moving, aiming for the gun flash. An indistinct figure moved just ahead of him, falling to the ground as he paused to take fresh aim. He went on, hoping that he was not exchanging fire with Walt Sand.

As he reached the street, shooting hammered out at his back. He paused, momentarily undecided. Riley was shooting rapidly, and shots were hammering from the street as Sand attempted to get into the office. Stafford bent over the man lying in the alley mouth but was unable to see much. He checked the figure and found it lifeless. Straightening, he peered around the corner into the street, and saw Sand immediately. The town marshal was standing at the broken window of the office, his gun flaming as he fired into the interior. Then Sand hurled himself headlong through the window, his gun still hammering.

Stafford went to the window, his movement coinciding with a lull in the shooting. He called Sand's name and the man appeared at the window, his face just a shapeless blur in the shadows. Sand was feeding fresh shells into his smoking gun. Stafford climbed into the office through the window.

'There was a couple of them in here,' Sand said. 'I nailed them.'

'I got one outside in the alley, and Riley was shooting at the rear. Open that door to the cells and we'll see what we've got.'

Sand nodded. Keys rattled as he opened the door. A gun crashed from the other side of the door and a bullet bored through the woodwork, passing between Stafford and Sand. Stafford kicked the door open and it struck a man standing in the passage on the other side. Sand's gun flashed and the man staggered, then fell. Two other guns opened fire from along the passage.

Stafford dropped flat and squirmed forward into the passage. Bullets hammered over him but he was not touched. He could see that the rear door of the jail was open, and two men were crouching just inside the doorway, exchanging shots with Riley, who was barring their escape.

Sand sent three shots along the passage and one

of the men by the door dropped instantly. Stafford shot the other, and then the shooting ceased. Echoes faded slowly. The jail was filled with choking gunsmoke.

'Hey there, inside the jail!' Riley bellowed from the darkness beyond the doorway. 'Can you hear me, Cleve?'

'I hear you,' Stafford replied. 'I figure we've cleared them between us. Did anyone get away?'

'Not since I've been here,' Riley retorted. 'I'm coming in.'

His big figure filled the doorway, blocking out what little light was filtering into the building from outside. Sand struck a match and lit a lamp suspended from a wall bracket. They looked around the smoky interior of the cell block. None of the cells had been opened, and all the prisoners were still inside.

Polder was standing at his door, gripping the bars, his eyes glinting in the lamplight. He met Stafford's gaze, his face harshly set.

'You've just lost six men, Polder,' Stafford said harshly. 'At the rate we're going, you'll have no one backing you come dawn.'

'I got no idea what you're talking about,' Polder snapped. 'I was under the impression they got in here to kill me.'

Stafford frowned, for that angle had not occurred to him. Polder saw his change of expression and laughed.

'I told you I know nothing of this crooked business,' he rapped. 'I guess you've got a lot to learn, Deputy.'

'We'll get at the truth in the morning,' Stafford replied. 'Let's make the place secure. Howie, bring in the man who was holding their horses, then bolt the back door. Let's get these bodies into the front office. It's time we took a real grip on this situation.'

'I reckon we've got it by the short and curlies,' Riley responded with a chuckle. 'Heck, we're knee-deep in dead hard cases.'

He went outside to return a moment later dragging the unconscious horse holder by the scruff of his neck. Sand unlocked an empty cell and Riley thrust the man inside. They dragged the three dead hard cases into the front office and laid them in a row with the two already lying there.

'There's another man in the alley mouth to the left,' Stafford said.

Riley went out to fetch the body, and was followed by Doc Wilson when he returned. Wilson's face was set in grim lines when he examined the bodies.

'Frank Willard won't be able to cope with the work you're creating for him,' the doctor observed. 'He was grumbling earlier about the men who have been killed since your arrival.'

'There's one in the cells you better look at, Doc,' Riley said cheerfully. 'All he's got is a bump on his head.'

'Thanks for the tip-off, Doc,' Stafford said.

'It was my pleasure.' Wilson spoke grimly. 'Come the morning, there won't be a hard case left in town.

I've heard tell how you cleaned out some of the pest-holes in the county, and you've sure proved the truth of what was said about you.'

'That's the way it goes.' Stafford nodded. 'Someone has to make a stand against the wrongdoers, and we seem suited to the job.'

Riley went to the window, where several towns-men were standing, looking into the office. Stafford glanced round when he heard their excited voices demanding news.

'Clear them out of there, Howie,' he said. 'I figure it's all over for tonight. It's about time the town settled down. It'll be sun-up in a few hours and then we'll be making a fresh start. I need some sleep, so if you're not going to sleep you can stand guard. Let's quieten the place and prepare for the next stage.'

Sand departed to make a round of the town and Riley posted himself by the window, watching the deserted street. Doc Wilson emerged from the cell block and went on his way. Stafford sat down at the desk and tried to write out a report, but within moments he lodged his elbows on the desk, propped his head in his hands, and slept. . . .

The sun shining in through a corner of the big front window threw a shaft of light into Stafford's face and he sat up instantly, rubbing his eyes. Riley was pacing the office, and paused at Stafford's move-ment. Stafford saw that the bodies had been removed. Walt Sand was seated on a chair by the door of the cell block, cleaning his guns.

'Cleve, I don't know how you can sleep with all the noise that's been going on,' Riley observed with a grin. 'But it's time you were awake. There's been a little guy in here from the eating house wanting to know how many breakfasts we need. I don't know about you, but I could eat a couple of helpings. All this law dealing sure hones a man's appetite.'

Stafford arose and stretched his cramped limbs.

'I made a round of the town just before first light,' Sand said. 'It's all quiet out there. In fact, I got a feeling it was too quiet, but that could have been my imagination.'

Stafford stifled a yawn. He felt gaunted inside, aware that he could have done with more sleep. But there was much to be done with the arrival of morning. He was tense, mentally poised for the ordeal that was awaiting them with the unfolding of the daylight hours. He was certain that their actions of the previous night had not cleared the town of its violent element.

A man appeared at the window and Sand drew his guns.

'Hold it,' Stafford rapped. 'It's Bill Harra.' He crossed to the window. 'What's on your mind, Bill?'

Harra's thin, angular face was lined with weariness but his blue eyes were gleaming. He glanced furtively around the street, his right hand down on his gun butt. When he spoke his voice was low-pitched, his words clipped and harsh.

'Mart Crayle is gathering men. He means to come and give you hell before the town is awake. They'll be the toughest men Polder's got. Be ready for them, Cleve. I got to get back before they miss me. I'll be with them when they come so what do you want me to do? Shall I take them from the rear when the shooting starts?'

'I think you'd better stay here with us right now,' Stafford replied. 'Come on inside, Bill. You've served us well.'

Harra nodded, and there was relief in his eyes as he entered the office. Stafford stood by the window looking out at the street. Sunlight was already probing the more obscure corners of the town. No one moved out there in the brooding silence. It would be another thirty minutes at least before the townsfolk stirred. And that was how Stafford liked it. It would suit him if this attack came in before the town was fully awake. He moved back to the desk and sat down to clean his weapons. The others were doing likewise. They were as ready as they could ever be.

# SEVEN

A noise on the street alerted them, and Riley sneaked a look out of the window. A bad-tempered voice began complaining noisily as boots thumped on the sidewalk outside the office door.

'It's the little guy with breakfast,' Riley reported.

Stafford went to the door and jerked it open. Bob Carmody, the café proprietor, had a small handcart outside loaded with metal receptacles containing breakfast.

'Hurry up and get that stuff inside,' Stafford rapped, 'then get out of here.'

Carmody cut off his flow of cursing and gazed at Stafford. His unkempt appearance and gaunted face would have been more suitable for a man who worked in a stable rather than the catering trade.

'You expecting trouble?' he demanded.

'Just do like you're told,' Stafford said.

Carmody busied himself, bringing in the food containers and placing them on the desk.

'Serve yourselves,' he said, bringing in some tin

99

plates. 'Don't worry about the empties. I'll collect them later.'

He left hurriedly and wheeled his handcart along the street almost at a run.

'Get that food served out and feed the prisoners,' Stafford said. He went to the window and glanced around the street, seeing a couple of men along the sidewalk who seemed to be loitering without good reason. 'We may get visitors at any moment,' he warned, and glanced at Harra, who was opening the breakfast containers, asking: 'Where are those gunnies gathering, Bill?'

'In Polder's saloon. Mart Crayle is bossing them. He's waiting for men to come in from Polder's ranches, and they're expected about now.'

'Mebbe we should try to catch them flat-footed,' Walt Sand said thoughtfully. 'If we dropped in on them before they were ready to come at us I reckon we could stop them in their tracks.'

'That's good reasoning,' Stafford nodded. 'But I wouldn't want to leave this place unguarded. If we had a few extra men we could stop this business here and now. Do you think you could handle this office alone, Walt? You're the town marshal, and I figure your place is here. If I took Riley and Harra, we could smash Polder's crooked game if we handled those hard cases.'

'Can we eat breakfast before we go?' Riley demanded. 'How much time do you figure we got, Bill?'

'Time enough to eat first,' Harra replied, ladling

food on to the plates. 'But you better hurry.'

The street door was pushed open and Stafford whirled, gun in hand. An old man stood in the doorway, clutching a stack of posters. He fell back a pace, blinking at the sight of the gun levelled at him.

'You said you wanted these posters first thing,' he said.

'Sure.' Stafford took a poster from the pile and looked at it, nodding as he read the stark notice that warned of imprisonment and a heavy fine as a penalty for carrying a gun inside town limits. 'Would you stick these up around town?' he asked. 'You'll be paid for your time. I want some posted in a prominent place at each end of the street, and enough around the street that nobody can fail to get the message.'

'I'll take care of that,' the man replied. 'It's all part of the job. But you'll have a tough time trying to make the by-law stick. And you better know that half a dozen riders just came into town and went into Polder's saloon. There's at least a dozen horses standing at the hitch-rails outside the place.'

'Thanks. Get those notices up soon as you can, then get off the street. Bill, Howie, let's go. We got work to do.'

Walt Sand was at the gun rack on the back wall. He took a twelve gauge shotgun from the rack and jerked open a small cupboard to pick up a box of cartridges. He looked at Stafford and grinned.

'You can leave this place to me,' he rasped. 'I'm all set now.'

Stafford nodded and went to the gun rack. He examined the long guns there, then handed a shotgun each to Riley and Harra before selecting one for himself. They each took a box of 12 gauge cartridges and loaded the fearsome, close-quarter weapons. Satisfied that they were ready, Stafford walked out to the street, followed closely by Riley and Harra. Riley went across the street to the opposite sidewalk and Harra stepped through the dust to the centre of the street. Stafford remained on the near sidewalk, and they started walking towards Polder's saloon, which was situated in the middle of the row of buildings on the left-hand side.

There were at least a dozen horses standing at hitching-rails in front of the saloon. Stafford looked around quickly, noting several men standing in front of the batwings. He signalled to Harra, who joined him.

'I figure we should try to get in the back door of the saloon,' he said.

'Just what I was thinking,' Harra grinned.

Stafford signalled to Riley and the big man came unhurriedly across the street. They entered an alley and made for the back lots, and now Stafford was in a hurry. He paused at the rear end of the alley and peered across the back lots, looking towards the saloon.

'I reckon they'll be ready for us,' Harra said.

'We ought to keep going and bust in on them.' Riley cocked his shotgun, eagerness sounding in his loud voice. 'They're probably having a drink to brace themselves. Let's go feed 'em some law, huh?'

'That's what we get paid for,' Stafford acknowledged. 'Let's go.'

'Gunsmoke for breakfast,' remarked Harra.

They left the alley and walked along the back lots, staying close to the rear of the buildings fronting the main street. Doc Wilson appeared from the back doorway of one of the buildings and started across the lots towards a small barn. He was carrying his medical bag. Spotting the three resolute lawmen, he pulled up short, frowning.

'Something happening?' he asked.

'Where are you going?' Stafford countered.

'I start early in the day. I need to check on Mrs McTaggart. She's expecting her second child any time now.'

'Mebbe you should stick around town a few minutes longer,' Stafford suggested. 'You could be needed pretty badly.'

'Sure.' The doc's face changed expression. 'I'll go back in the house and make that cup of coffee I didn't have time for a couple of minutes ago. I'll know when I'm needed, huh?'

Stafford smiled and went on. Riley and Harra flanked him closely. They reached the rear door of the saloon and Stafford grasped the handle, which turned as he touched it. The door was pulled open from the inside and a man began to emerge. Stafford palmed his Colt and slammed the long barrel against the side of the man's head. Riley leaned forward and grasped the limp figure as it slumped to the ground. Harra snatched a gun from the man's holster and stuck it into his own waistband.

Entering the building, Stafford found himself in a passage. Several doors were spaced along either side, all closed, and he did not bother to check the rooms he passed. He made for the door that led into the bar, crowded by his two companions. Opening the door silently, he glanced at his men, who nodded, and then went through the doorway, shotgun levelling for action as he passed under the wide staircase and the long bar came into view. The batwings were off to the right.

There were at least a dozen men in the bar, and three were standing just outside the batwings, watching the street. Two men stood behind the bar, handing out drinks, and the rest were lining the bar, drinking freely.

Stafford paused, gun levelled, and Riley and Harra moved up beside him, one either side, guns cocked and covering the men. They moved apart slightly, Harra on Stafford's left and Riley on the right. Stafford went forward a couple of paces, then planted his feet firmly on the sanded boards. He drew his six-gun and fired a shot into the back of the bar above the heads of the assembled men, and his gun went back into its holster before the echoes of the shot began to fade. He tightened his grip on the shotgun, earing back the hammers, waiting for a reaction to his shot.

The men at the bar froze in that first moment, then came whirling around, some instinctively reaching for their guns.

'Stand still!' Stafford yelled. 'This is the law. Hands up, all of you.'

The men froze, some with hands on their gun butts. All were tense, hair-triggered for action.

'Get your hands away from your guns,' Stafford rapped.

One of the men behind the bar ducked below the counter, then reappeared with a gun in his hand. He fired at Stafford from between two men in front of the bar and his bullet plucked at Stafford's hatbrim. The shot triggered the other men into action. Without exception, they reached for their guns.

Stafford fired the shotgun, its booming roar hammering out the silence. Three men in front of him went sprawling sideways blasted by the heavy buckshot from the fearsome weapon. Blue gunsmoke speared across the saloon, and then Harra and Riley were shooting, covering the rest of the men at the bar. Six loads of buckshot tore into the closely-packed group before they could get their guns working, and they fell to the floor in a welter of spurting blood.

Stafford drew his six-gun and shot one of the men behind the counter. Harra got the second man there, Riley half-turned to his right, facing the batwings, and triggered his drawn Colt at the men who came bursting into the saloon from the sidewalk. Two appeared together, and went down with flailing arms. A third thrust open the batwings, gun in hand, and both Stafford and Harra shot him. He sprawled backwards and fell limply on the sidewalk.

Stafford's ears were singing from the crash of shooting in such close confines. The air was thick with the stench of burned powder. He looked at the sprawled bodies in front of the bar and fought down a wave of nausea that threatened to overwhelm him. This carnage went with the badge he was wearing, but he had never become accustomed to it. And there were times when it seemed too much of a burden to tolerate.

Harra placed his shotgun on top of the bar and looked at the two men lying behind it. Both were dead. He transferred his attention to the clustered men in front of the bar. Most were dead, but he found three who were still breathing and dragged them forward for attention.

Riley went to the batwings and glanced outside. He turned and looked at Stafford. 'It's all clear out there,' he reported. 'We got 'em cold.'

Stafford went to the batwings and stepped outside for some fresh air. His keen gaze swept around the street. Men were emerging from their homes, attracted by the thunderous reports of the shooting, and Doc Wilson was already coming along the sidewalk, bag in hand. Stafford waited until the doctor arrived, then motioned for him to enter the saloon. He followed the doctor into the building.

Wilson halted in shock and Stafford heard him mutter under his breath.

'These three are still alive, Doc,' Harra said. 'The others have all cashed their chips.'

Riley had removed weapons from the dead men

and piled them on the bar. He was busy dragging the corpses into some semblance of a line, and when he had completed the grisly chore he added the three men who had run into the saloon. When he had finished he walked to Stafford's side.

'It was better to deal with them in here than at the law office,' he said.

Stafford nodded. 'And we gave them the chance to surrender.' He turned to Harra, who was standing at the end of the bar with the butt of his shotgun tucked in his right armpit.

'Which one is Mart Crayle, Bill?' he called.

'This one.' Harra walked to the three wounded men and kicked the foot of one of them. 'I had to listen to him half the night, talking about what he was gonna do to you this morning. But it didn't work out his way, huh? It seems to me that we've knocked the fight out of Polder's bunch. What's on the cards now, Cleve?'

'I want to take a look around town,' Stafford replied. 'You better stay here in case the Doc wants anything. When I get back we'll see about gathering evidence against Polder. Then we'll enforce the law banning firearms inside town limits. I'll take Howie with me.'

'Sure thing.' Harra walked behind the bar. 'Do you need a drink before you go?'

'No.' Stafford shook his head. He felt the need for fresh air, and motioned to Riley as he left the saloon. On the sidewalk he paused and looked around, finding himself in a crowd of about twenty excited

townsmen. Eager voices demanded news of what
had happened inside the saloon. Stafford motioned
for the crowd to give ground and they backed off,
gazing at the shotgun he was carrying. He saw little
knots of men standing around farther along the
sidewalk, some of them looking at the posters being
put up.

'We're gonna need to make some arrangements
for the guns that will be handed in at the office,' he
said to Riley, pushing through the crowd and starting along the sidewalk.

Riley fell into step beside him and they walked
towards the town limits. Tom Harper, the printer,
was at this end of town and they saw him nailing a
poster to the wall of the livery barn. As Harper
moved away, two men came out of the barn and
paused to read the poster. Both were wearing guns.
Stafford and Riley reached them as the men
finished digesting the information, and one man
dropped a hand to his holstered gun and shrugged
his thick shoulders.

'There ain't nobody in this town gonna take my
gun off me,' he declared. 'Just let them try.'

'That ain't the attitude to take,' Riley boomed,
startling both men. 'And you don't have to go far
around here to find someone who can take that
hogleg off you.'

Both men turned, and froze at the sight of
Stafford and Riley, both carrying shotguns. Riley
grinned.

'It don't pay to shoot off your mouth until you've

had a chance to look at the opposition. What's your business here?'

'We're riding through,' one of them replied. 'We don't want no trouble. We've stopped for a drink and a bite to eat while our horses are being fed and rested, that's all.'

'Not wearing guns,' Riley boomed. 'Get rid of them. You got saddle-bags, so stow them away. You won't need guns around here.'

Stafford had remained silent and watchful while Riley handled the situation. The two men went back into the stable to emerge some moments later minus their guns and holsters. Riley approached the man who had voiced his protest at going disarmed, and slapped him lightly around the midriff, searching for a hidden weapon. He reached around to check the man's back, and felt the outline of a pistol butt under the shirt just above the waistline.

'You're sure asking for trouble,' Riley rasped, dragging the man's shirt out of his pants and grasping the butt of the gun. He waved the big weapon under the man's nose. 'What makes you so sure you don't have to obey the law like everyone else?' He looked suspiciously at the second man and demanded pugnaciously: 'Are you carrying a hideout gun?'

The man produced a six-gun from under his shirt and Riley snatched it.

'You two are gonna see the inside of our jail,' he rasped. 'On your way. Straight along the sidewalk to the other end of town. We're gonna make an example of you.'

They herded the men through town, and some of the crowd waiting outside the saloon began to follow behind in the hope of seeing some action. Bill Harra emerged from the saloon and fell into step beside Stafford.

'The doc has got his end of the business under control,' Harra reported. 'But Willard, the under-taker, is getting hot under his collar. Too many dead men to handle.'

'He should worry,' Stafford grimaced. 'But I got the feeling that we've just about busted the crooked set-up in town. What we need now is evidence against Polder. Once we've got that roped and hog-tied we can leave the town to Walt Sand and get to grips with the rustling. Did you hear any mention of it while you were around with Polder's hard cases?'

Harra shook his head. 'No. Just general talk, and I figure that to be strange. When I brought up the subject, Mart Crayle ignored it, although he had mentioned it earlier. Maybe Polder has a gang of rustlers out at one of his spreads, if he is responsible for the cattle stealing.'

'Shemp will have some information for us by the time we're ready to hit the range,' Stafford said confidently. 'I'll want you and Howie on the street this morning, Bill. Sand will need some help making the gun law stick, if these two jaspers are anything to go by.'

'Some of the townsmen are armed,' Harra said, glancing around at the crowd. 'I guess wearing a gun has become a part of life around here.'

'But not any more,' Stafford said.

They reached the law office with at least a score of townsmen following them, and when they entered the office with the prisoners the clamour of excited voices outside rose in volume. Some of the townsmen crowded around the broken window, eager to witness everything that was going on.

'Howie, disperse that crowd,' Stafford ordered. 'And warn the men that the gun law takes immediate effect. They've got ten minutes to get rid of their guns. After that we arrest everyone defying the order.'

Riley grinned and went out to the street. His loud voice soon quietened the crowd and he warned them off. They began to drift away, some of them removing their gunbelts as they did so.

Walt Sand was sitting at the desk, and he eyed the two prisoners. He got to his feet and reached for the cell keys.

'Charge them with carrying guns in town, knowing it to be an offence,' Stafford said.

'Where are we gonna put all the offenders?' Sand demanded. 'The cells are almost overflowing now, and there are some wounded men at the doctor's place who will be coming along here shortly. We're gonna need a temporary jail until you can come up with an answer to the problem.'

'I'll talk to the town mayor and see about getting a special court to sit in judgement on the offenders,' Stafford said. 'They'll be fined and released. Once we get the system up and running it'll take care of itself. Polder and his men are another matter. We've got to get evidence against Polder and make it stick.'

Sand nodded. He unlocked the door leading into the cells. The prisoners were ushered into the remaining unoccupied cell, and Stafford walked to the cell where Polder was seated on a bunk. Polder was looking gaunt and untidy. He met Stafford's gaze with an unblinking stare.

'You got anything to say for yourself this morning, Polder?' Stafford asked. 'The evidence against you is piling up. If you've got any defence at all then you better spill it so we can get on with the case.'

'I got nothing to say to you about anything,' Polder replied. 'I want to see Ward. He'll get me out of here in two minutes flat.'

Stafford grinned. 'We don't see eye to eye on that,' he said. 'It's gonna be a long time before you walk out of here. I got you pegged as being the man back of the trouble in town. And when I start looking around for rustlers out on the range I expect to find that you're behind it. I've already got witnesses who are prepared to swear that you cheated some of the small ranchers out of their spreads and committed murder in the process. You've got a lot of thinking to do, Polder, and your best bet is to come clean about the whole shebang.'

'Hey, Cleve!' Riley called loudly from the office. 'Come out here, will you?'

Stafford gazed into Polder's eyes for a moment, wondering which way the saloonman would jump. But Polder merely shook his head and turned away.

Stafford was aware that time was on his side, and went back to the office.

'What's on your mind, Howie?' he demanded.

'Out here,' the big deputy said harshly, moving to the street door.

Frowning, Stafford walked out to the sidewalk. A pang struck through him when he recognized the trail-weary horse that was standing at the hitch rail, head drooping, and lying in the dust beside the animal was the small figure of Shemp Peck. The little deputy was unconscious, and ominous stains of blood showed starkly on his pale shirt. . . .

# EIGHT

Stafford ran forward and dropped to one knee beside the inert figure of Shemp Peck. Examining his sidekick, he was relieved to find that Peck was still alive. The little deputy had been shot in the back, the bullet emerging through the front of his left shoulder.

'I've sent for the doc,' Riley said worriedly. 'Will he make it, Cleve?'

'He's a tough little cuss.' Stafford spoke through gritted teeth. He ripped open Peck's blood-soaked shirt to reveal a large, ragged hole in the little deputy's left shoulder just below the collar bone. Dried blood had matted around the wound and a thin trickle of fresh blood was oozing from its centre.

'Looks like he took that slug some hours ago,' Riley observed. 'Let's look at his back. This is the exit wound. If the entrance hole ain't too low then he'll be all right.'

'Let's leave him lie until the doc gets here,' Stafford suggested.

114

'He's coming now.' Riley was watching the street. 'This is one hell of a play, Cleve. You shouldn't have let Shemp ride out on his own. I could have gone with him.'

'Shemp knew enough to keep out of trouble.' Stafford spoke harshly, already wishing he had sent Riley with the little deputy. He moved back when Doc Wilson arrived hurriedly, medical bag in hand.

The doctor dropped to his knees in the dust and examined Peck. 'Give me a hand and we'll sit him up,' he said curtly. 'I need to check his back.'

Riley stepped forward and gently eased Peck into a sitting position. Stafford watched stolidly. A crowd was gathering around them.

'Looks like he took a 44.40 slug,' Wilson observed.

'Winchester,' Riley said harshly. 'Shot in the back from cover. Someone sure was shooting first and asking questions afterwards. Hell, I can't wait to get out on the range after those rustlers. We'll give 'em trouble when we get among them.'

Doc Wilson arose and addressed the crowd. 'Four of you pick him up and carry him to my place,' he instructed. 'Take it easy. He can't afford to lose any more blood.' He looked at Stafford. 'Look in on me in about an hour. I'll be finished with him by then. But I figure he'll pull through, barring complications.'

'Thanks, Doc,' Stafford nodded. 'You've been pretty busy since I hit town, huh? But I reckon we've just about cleaned up around here.' He looked around at the crowd, noting that some of the men were wearing guns. Raising his voice, he addressed them. 'If you haven't read the posters going up around town then you better do so now. In an hour we'll be checking the town, and anyone found carrying a gun will be jailed and fined.'

Four men picked up the slight figure of Shemp Peck and walked slowly along the street with Doc Wilson in attendance. The crowd began to disperse. Stafford heaved a sigh as he turned to examine Peck's horse, which showed signs of having been hard ridden.

'Howie, take this horse along to the livery barn and rub him down. Then move around town checking for armed men. Don't arrest anyone yet unless you get trouble. We'll issue warnings for an hour or so to make sure everyone knows about the posters.'

'When are we gonna hit the range?' Riley demanded. 'I wanta come up with the guy who shot Shemp.'

'We'll make sure things are under control around here before we saddle and ride. But it won't be long before we hit those rustlers.'

Riley led Peck's weary horse along the street. Stafford stood for a moment, trying to relax, feeling the pace of the law dealing he had administered since his arrival. But he was satisfied with his progress. The town was practically in the hands of the law, and while Polder was behind bars there was no way the crooked saloonman could organize further resistance.

'You wanted a statement from me, ' a voice said at Stafford's shoulder, and he turned swiftly to see Ira

Benson standing on the sidewalk. 'You've sure been busy cleaning up the town.'

'You own the B Bar B ranch, huh?' Stafford asked.

Benson nodded. 'Is Polder still in jail? Can you make your kind of law stick around here?'

'Yeah. Polder is still behind bars, and likely to stay there for a long time. But I need evidence to keep him there. Come into the office and we'll talk. If you can throw any light on the local rustling, I'll be pleased to hear about it.'

'I've seen men I know are in Polder's pay hazing stolen stock across the range,' Benson said as they entered the law office. 'And I told you last night that Polder is behind the ranch-grabbing that's been going on. I'll make a statement only if you can assure me that Polder won't get out of jail and turn on me for opening my mouth. If you can promise that then you'll find other Polder victims ready to talk.'

'That's good news. There's also that business in the saloon last night to be sorted out. My deputy saw the gambler, Sheldon, cheating, and he'll give evidence about that. I want to be able to prove that Sheldon was cheating you and other ranchers so that Polder could buy you out cheaply.' Stafford looked at Walt Sand, who was seated at the desk. 'Will you take down Benson's statement, Walt?'

'Sure thing. You ain't left me much to do around town now most of the gunnies are dead or behind bars.' Sand grinned, but his face sobered when Ward, the lawyer, appeared in the doorway. 'If you're hoping to spring Polder this morning then you better think again,' he said harshly. 'We're in the process of gathering evidence, and Polder will be charged soon as we get a straight picture of what's been going on around here.'

Ward set his leather case on a corner of the desk and opened it. 'I've been making some enquiries myself,' he retorted. 'I've learned that certain men on the range are responsible for the rustling, and they've been throwing the blame on to my client. One of the rustlers is standing here right now, no doubt giving lying testament against Griff Polder.'

'You calling me a rustler?' Benson demanded fiercely. 'Well, if that don't beat all! But that's what I would expect from Polder, and anyone who works for him.' He looked at Stafford. 'The law will have to make up its mind about who is telling the truth. But I can do better than just accuse Polder of running the rustling. Me and some of my neighbours can take you to a place where rustled Big T and M Bar stock are being held until a sizeable herd has been gathered to trail to the markets in the north.'

'Let's get all the accusations down on paper,' Stafford said, 'then we can decide what to do.'

'Here are two statements.' Ward placed several sheets of paper on the desk. 'I suggest you release my client until you have something to charge him with. He's an influential man in this county, and won't abscond. If you need him, he'll be right here, running his legal businesses.'

Stafford smiled. 'I got enough on Polder now to hold him on several charges. He ain't going anywhere, so ease off. You're wasting your time here, so haul it. We got work to do and don't need time-wasters hanging around.'

'I'll see Judge Pennington, get a court order for Polder to be released, and you'll get sued for wrong-ful arrest.'

'If you don't get out of here you could find yourself the wrong side of the bars,' Stafford said impa-tiently.

Ward stood his ground for a moment, then shook his head and departed. Sand grinned at the lawyer's discomfiture. He motioned for Benson to sit down and began to write out the rancher's statement. Stafford went to the street door and looked around. The town was wide awake, its inhabitants thronging the street to learn the latest news of the situation. He noted that most of the men had divested them-selves of their firearms.

He went back to the desk and picked up the state-ments the lawyer had left. They were signed by Jake Berle and Pete Johnson. Both statements were simi-larly worded, stating that a number of the smaller ranchers were responsible for the rustling.

'Do you know Berle and Johnson?' Stafford asked Benson.

'I sure do.' Benson spoke in a ragged tone. 'They run the two spreads that Polder took over recently from my neighbours. They're the men I've seen hazing other ranchers' cattle across the range. You don't need to look any further than them to find the rustlers.'

'You better ride with us when we leave town,' Stafford decided. 'I'll need a man along who knows the range. I want to ride out in about an hour. But first I'll take a turn around the town to check it out. It seems quiet, and I need to check with the mayor before I leave to see if I've missed any of Polder's men.'

He left the office and went along the street, answering many questions asked by the townsmen. He warned several of them to take off their guns, and paused when he reached the doctor's house. Several men were standing in a group, discussing the events of the night, and one of them told Stafford that Wilson had said Shemp Peck would be all right.

The undertaker, Frank Willard, and his assistant, came along the street with a buckboard. Stafford walked behind the vehicle to the saloon, where Bill Harra was standing at the batwings. Willard was beefing about the workload facing him.

'You'd better make the most of it while you can,' Harra laughed. 'You could die of hunger when we get through here and the town returns to normal.' His face sobered when he turned to Stafford. 'I heard about Shemp,' he said. 'How is he doing?'

'Doc Wilson says he'll be all right.' Stafford glanced around the street. 'I'll check with him shortly. We'll be riding out soon, to hit the rustlers. Take a turn around the street now, Bill, and warn anyone you see wearing a gun to take it off. The law will come into effect before we leave, and Walt Sand will enforce it. I'm gonna check with the mayor. He should know if any hard cases are left in town. I want them all behind bars before we leave. Saddle our horses in about an hour and bring them along to the jail, huh? We need to strike fast, before the rustlers get word that the town has been cleaned out.'

'Sure thing.' Harra moved off along the sidewalk.

Stafford went in the opposite direction and entered the Mercantile, pausing in the doorway to glance around the shadowed interior. Pete Boxall was already behind the counter, serving a female customer. He spotted Stafford, and came towards the door, an expansive smile on his lined face, although his eyes showed tension.

'Morning,' he greeted. 'You haven't wasted any time in cleaning out the town. I didn't expect the job to be done inside of a week. Every time I heard shooting I told myself that the law was here to stay.'

'That's what I want to talk to you about.' Stafford moved to one side of the doorway from force of habit. 'You're a local man, and being the mayor means that you have a finger on the town's pulse. I want you to check on the men we've put out of action so far, then tell me if there are men around who should be investigated. Me and my pards are riding out shortly to tackle the rustling, and we wanta leave the town with a clean bill of health. I don't want any loose ends left untied.'

'Sure. I'll get my wife to tend the store while I go with you.'

Stafford nodded and went outside to stand on the sidewalk looking around. Boxall joined him shortly, having divested himself of his apron in favour of a black jacket. As he emerged from the store, the mayor looked around the street as if expecting gunmen to spring out at him.

'Have you got charges against Polder yet?' he asked. 'I reckon it will be hard to nail him. He's thumbed his nose at the law for a long time, although everyone knew he was behind the crookedness.'

'Evidence is being collected. Men are beginning to loosen up. They can see that the law has the upper hand, and when they're convinced that Polder can't come back they'll really open up. What I need from you, with your local knowledge, is whether I've missed anyone in Polder's set-up. Come along to the jail and take a look at the prisoners, and if you can name anyone in town who should be with them then I'll be pleased to know about it.'

They went to the jail, where a carpenter had started work on replacing the broken front window. A crowd was still waiting in front of the law office, evidently expecting more violent developments in the law's fight for supremacy over the badmen.

Boxall was silent as he walked through the crowded cell-block looking at the prisoners. He remained silent even when Polder spoke to him, and ignored the pleas from some of the hard cases who professed innocence and begged him for help. When they returned to the front office, the mayor heaved a sigh of relief. He nodded when meeting Stafford's incisive gaze, and his tension seemed to have dissipated.

'It looks like you've got everyone connected with Polder,' he said. 'You've done a fine job, and I hope your business on the range goes as well.'

'Keep your eyes open around here, and tell Sand if you see anyone who should be behind bars.' Stafford went out to the sidewalk to check the street and Boxall accompanied him. 'I'll be riding out pretty soon,' he added.

A shot crashed out, sending echoes along the broad street. Stafford spun on his heel, hand dropping to the butt of his holstered gun. He saw Riley, gun in hand, bending over an inert figure, and relaxed when Bill Harra appeared from the livery barn leading three saddled horses. Harra mounted to go to Riley's side. Evidently someone had objected to being disarmed.

'Yes, sir,' Boxall commented. 'You've tamed this town in a matter of hours.'

'Make sure you back up your town marshal,' Stafford told him. 'Help him keep the law on top.'

Boxall departed and Stafford went back into the office. Sand had finished taking Benson's statement, and he grinned at Stafford.

'We got enough here to put Polder away for a lifetime,' he said exultantly.

'You can check my story with other ranchers,'

Benson said. 'I'll fetch my horse, huh? We ought to be getting out on the range to grab the proof you'll need. Polder's hard cases will be moving out with that herd any time now.'

'Yes. Saddle up and we'll ride.' Stafford experienced a pang of impatience to hit the trail. 'My men are almost ready to leave. I just need to check on Shemp Peck and get his report, if he's able to give it.'

He went back to the street and Sand accompanied him. They watched Benson walk along the sidewalk towards the livery barn. The town seemed to overwhelm Stafford, and he felt a deep yearning for the wide open spaces. 'Are you happy that you can handle the town?' he asked, and Sand nodded.

'You've smoked out most of the troublemakers. I reckon I can handle it until my two sidekicks arrive. They should be here some time today.'

'You'd better get a couple of honest townsmen in here to help hold the place in case Polder's men on the range decide to come in and bust him loose.' Stafford's tone was gentle, but there was grim reality in his voice.

Sand nodded. 'You bet. I ain't never lost a prisoner and I don't intend to start now. There'll be a couple of jailers in here shortly.'

Riley came breezing into the office, a wide grin on his fleshy face. 'Did you hear that shot?' he demanded. 'Some galoot reached for his gun the minute I spoke to him. I didn't have a chance to do anything but bore him. The doc is taking care of him, and he'll live to add to the overcrowding in here. But most of the townsmen are going along with the order, Cleve. I get the impression that they'll be happy to leave their guns at home so long as they can rely on the law to keep troublemakers under control. Bill's got the horses, so I guess we're about to ride, huh?'

Harra looked into the office. 'All ready,' he announced. 'The horses are fit to travel.'

'We'll hit the saddle when Benson shows up,' Stafford decided. 'Better get in some supplies, Bill, and cartridges. There's no telling how long we'll be out on the range. I figure the rustlers are pretty well covered up, and we might have a tough chore digging them out. I wanta check on Shemp, so take care of the supplies, huh?'

He went along the street to the doctor's house. There was still a crowd standing on the sidewalk, and Stafford was pleased to see that none of them was armed. He knocked at the door and Doc Wilson opened it, smiling a welcome.

'You'll be happy to learn that your man will pull through,' he said. 'But he's gonna be out of action for at least a month.'

'That's good news.' Stafford was heartened by the doctor's words. 'Is he conscious? I need to know what he discovered out on the range.'

Wilson shook his head. 'He hasn't come round yet. I had to put him out to work on him. The bullet missed his vital spots, but he was dusted both sides, and, barring infection, he'll make a good recovery. But you won't be able to talk to him for hours.'

'I need to make tracks immediately,' Stafford mused. 'When he does wake up get Walt Sand to question him. If Shemp has anything to report, Sand can send a rider out to us. I'll arrange it with him. Thanks for all your help, Doc. We couldn't have done it so fast on our own.'

'I'm glad I was able to be of some help,' Wilson replied. 'I wish you luck against the rustlers.'

Stafford nodded and departed. He went back to the law office and talked with the town marshal. Benson was waiting inside, his horse tied to the hitch rail out front. Riley emerged from the cell block.

'Let's ride along to the store and chase up Bill,' Stafford said. 'We should be hitting the trail now. This job is only half finished, and time is wasting away.'

He led the way outside. Riley and Benson sided him when he swung into his saddle and they started along the street. As they reached the front of the store the sound of rapidly approaching hoofs shattered the peacefulness. Stafford twisted in his saddle and saw half a dozen riders coming into town at a fast clip. He recognized Ben Tudman leading them, and the Big T rancher was holding a six-gun.

Tudman spotted Stafford and pulled his horse down to a walk. Silence returned as the six riders came forward. Stafford tensed, wondering what developments had occurred on the range. The Big T outfit looked primed for trouble, and Stafford spotted one man, with blood stains on his shirt front, being supported by a companion. He was reeling in his saddle and looked badly wounded. Ben Tudman's fleshy face looked as if it had been carved out of rock, and he waved his drawn six-gun as he confronted Stafford.

'What kind of law are you running?' he demanded angrily. 'You're sitting around town while rustlers are killing my men and stealing me blind.'

'Calm down,' Stafford rapped. 'And put away that gun. We're on our way to check on the rustling. If you've had trouble with rustlers then give me the facts. We're gonna need all the help we can get.'

Tudman thrust his gun into its holster and turned to give orders to his men. Two of them helped the wounded man along the street to the doctor's house. The remaining two dismounted and stood watching the street as if expecting trouble to jump them.

'So what's happened?' Stafford demanded.

Tudman dismounted and leaned against his horse. He looked to be in the final stages of exhaustion. Covered in dust, his face was grey, lined with tension.

'My place was hit last night by around twenty rustlers,' he rapped. 'They came helling into my yard like a bunch of Indians on the warpath, shooting and screeching. They burned down the barn and killed four of my men before running off a herd of five hundred steers. We gave chase, but they were too strong for us, so I cut my losses and came on here for help. If you wanta catch the rustlers then you won't get a better chance than this. All hell has busted loose on the range.'

'You would have been strong enough to fight them off if you'd done as I suggested and teamed up with M Bar,' Stafford said grimly. 'I warned you two ranchers last night to get together.'

'Is that so?' Tudman straightened wearily and dropped a hand to his holstered gun. 'We managed to knock some of the rustlers out of their saddles, and downed two of their mounts. When I checked their horses I found M Bar branded on them, and one of the dead men was recognized as an M Bar rider. I guess that puts Charlie Martin on the spot. I've suspected him all along of running the rustling, and now I got the proof I need. That's why I'm here instead of being at M Bar. I want the law with me when I call on Martin for a showdown.'

Stafford stepped down from his saddle, considering Tudman's grim words. He had thought the law's work was almost finished, but now it seemed that it had only just begun. . . .

# NINE

A crowd began to form in front of the store, talking excitedly about the new developments. Stafford spoke to Tudman.

'We'll be splitting the breeze shortly, and you'll need fresh horses if you want to stay up with us. Go get them, and be ready to ride when we reach the livery barn.'

Tudman turned away, staggering wearily, and Stafford's thoughts were bleak as he considered the task ahead. He swung into his saddle and rode along the street to the law office. Walt Sand came to the open doorway when he heard the rapidly approaching hoofs, and Stafford told the town marshal what he had learned.

'You'd better take a posse with you,' Sand said. 'Charlie Martin owns a big spread, and if he's guilty he'll put up a fight.'

Stafford shook his head. 'I'll have enough men to handle the job I want to do,' he decided. 'If any of the M Bar outfit ride into town then stick them behind bars until I get back.'

'Sure thing,' Sand nodded grimly. 'Watch your back out there on the range.'

Stafford reined about and went back to the store. Harra was tying a sack of supplies to his cantle and Riley was fastening a smaller sack behind his saddle. Harra handed Stafford a box of .45 cartridges for his pistol and a box of 44.40 calibre cartridges for his Winchester. They rode along the street to the livery barn, and reached it as Ben Tudman emerged, leading a fresh horse.

Tudman climbed into his saddle and rode to Stafford's side. His four men appeared from the barn and joined them, leading fresh horses. Tudman seemed like a man who had taken on too many troubles. His face was dusty, beaded with sweat, and he looked as if he hadn't slept in a week.

'We'd better head for my place,' Tudman said. 'It's the nearest point from here, and you'll need to see the evidence. I don't figure you'll take my word for anything.'

'That sounds fine to me,' Stafford nodded. 'Lead the way with your men and we'll tag along.'

Tudman nodded and spoke to his men. They rode out of town at a fast clip, heading north, and Stafford followed closely, flanked by his two deputies. Ira Benson sided him and they left town in a cloud of dust.

Clear of the town, they crossed a river which was knee-high in thick brush. Tudman was trying to set a fast pace, but the horses had to pick their way past rocks and over sand bars that glared brilliant white in the morning sun. Then they hit the undulating range, heading north, and hammered through a stand of cottonwoods. They emerged on to a flat, where clumps of sagebrush and greasewood grew belly-high to a horse.

Nobody spoke. They rode too fast for that. Leaving the river area, they struck a rocky stretch that gave way eventually to a row of flat-topped hills, following a well-defined trail across a network of creek beds and dry washes. The horses had to push through numerous patches of low, thorny brushwood. The morning heat increased as the sun crossed the high blue vault of the sky, ascending to its apex.

They continued without a break, and the sun was in its high-noon position when Stafford finally spotted a ranch headquarters in the middle distance. Tudman did not spare the horses, and they rode on into a wide yard. Stafford reined in beside two dead animals horses lying in the thick dust. Tudman had dismounted beside the horses and stood waiting for Stafford to join him. He pointed to the brands on the animals.

'M Bar,' he said, shaking his head. 'I always had my doubts about Charlie Martin.'

'You could be jumping to conclusions,' Stafford observed harshly. 'These animals might have been stolen from M Bar.'

'Whose side are you on?' Tudman's fleshy face became suffused with anger.

'I'm on nobody's side. I represent the law and have

to look at a situation from more than one angle. It wouldn't do for me to go off half-cocked. What do you want me to do, ride down Martin and kill him for rustling? And before you answer, consider this from the other angle. If these horses were in Martin's yard with your brand on them, would you be happy if I rode in here shooting first and asking questions afterwards?'

Tudman shook his head. 'I guess you're right,' he said reluctantly. 'What are you gonna do?'

'We'll get up with the rustled herd and see what we can grab. You better stay here on your spread until I get back to you. I don't want any complications when I meet up with the rustlers.'

'You'll need gun help if you do catch up with them,' Tudman said aggressively.

'We've fought rustlers before,' Bill Harra commented. 'We'd, better water the horses before we move out.'

'There's a water trough in that corral.' Tudman pointed across the yard.

Harra dismounted and took the reins of Stafford's horse, leading it with his own animal to the corral. Riley went with him, taking Benson's horse.

'You'll find tracks of the herd over there.' Tudman pointed north. 'Heading north-east.'

'That's the direction of the place I told you about,' Benson cut in. 'I don't know about Martin's outfit being responsible for this rustling, but more than once I've seen Polder's men trailing stolen stock over that way.'

'We'll head out soon as the horses have been watered,' Stafford said.

They rode on minutes later, and Stafford felt uneasy as they headed away from Big T. He glanced back over his shoulder several times after the ranch had disappeared into the background, and finally grunted in satisfaction.

'You got something on your mind, Cleve?' Riley demanded. He was sweating profusely, his red shirt dark with perspiration.

'Yeah. I didn't expect Tudman to stay out of this. He's following us at a distance, so don't relax. Trouble could come at us from any direction. Set a good pace, Benson, and head straight for the place where the rustlers are holding the stolen stock, even if these tracks don't lead to it. We can always come back to Tudman's herd.'

Benson nodded and moved out into the lead. There were low hills ahead and he headed for them. The trail left by the stolen herd led in the same direction. Stafford was glad they didn't have to cast around for tracks. But this was appearing to be too easy, and there were many reservations in his mind.

By the middle of the afternoon they were riding through rough ground, still following the tracks of the stolen herd. Hills cut down their range of vision, and Stafford was concerned that this was perfect ambush country. He wondered how Benson had found the place he was making for. Rustlers would have hidden their stolen stock very well, and blotted the trail they inevitably left. But very soon the ground turned rocky and the tracks were no longer apparent.

They paused frequently to rest their tiring horses, and Stafford voiced some of the questions uppermost in his mind. He dismounted and stood beside Ira Benson, who was gazing ahead with eyes that were introspective, seeing not the country they were crossing but the distant place where he had found the rustlers' hideout.

'Benson, how did you manage to find their roost?' Stafford demanded.

'The rustlers stole stock from me and Pete McGovern, and I stuck to the trail until I found the roost.'

'And you did nothing about it?' Stafford watched Benson's impassive face, but saw no outward indication of what the man was thinking because his expression was like that of a professional gambler.

'I did what I could. I approached all my neighbours and tried to raise a group that would get the cattle back. But no one wanted to get involved. It was too dangerous, they said.'

'So what did you do?'

Benson laughed gratingly. 'There was nothing I could do. You know what the law was like in Concho before you rode in.'

'You could have got word to Sheriff Arlen.'

Benson shook his head. 'Nope. Word might have got out what I had done, and those rustlers would have found it easy to hit my place and kill me and my family.'

Stafford nodded. 'Yeah, I guess you're right. But you're out here now, and we will force a showdown with the rustlers. You're certain the thieves you saw were some of Polder's men?'

'Certain sure! I've seen enough of them riding around the spreads scaring folks into selling out.'

'So how far is it now to the roost?' Impatience was tugging at Stafford's mind.

'About two hours.' Benson squinted at the sun. 'We'll get there just before sundown.'

'That'll be fine.' Stafford had to be satisfied. 'Let's go on.'

They mounted and continued. The ground became even more broken and rough, and they had to ride through dry washes and draws that cut into the high ground. The tracks left by the stolen herd showed here and there, and they continued unerringly, but their progress on the upward slope was slow.

Stafford was leading with Benson on his left when a rider came down the faint trail at breakneck speed, unexpectedly rounding a large rock which had blotted out all sounds of his approach. Stafford pulled his horse aside to avoid a collision, but there was no space for manoeuvre and the rider caught him a glancing blow, yelling in surprise.

Stafford had reacted instinctively, pulling his left foot out of the stirrup and swinging out of the saddle as the newcomer's horse scraped his own. The stranger hauled on his reins, almost lifting his animal clear of disaster, but the horse side-swiped a protruding rock on the opposite side of the defile and went down in a threshing heap, throwing the rider over its head.

Stafford dropped his reins and ran forward to where the newcomer was in a daze on hands and knees, shaking his head. He grasped the man's shoulder and dragged him upright, snatching a pistol from his holster even as the man reached for it. The man staggered, and would have fallen if Riley had not come forward and grasped him in an unbreakable grip.

'Well what do you know?' Riley boomed. 'Look who's dropped in for a little chat? It's Abe Strother, Tudman's foreman. What are you doing in this neck of the woods, Strother, and in such a hurry?'

Strother blinked and then shrugged his heavy shoulders. Despite his large size he was outweighed by Howard Riley.

'Heck, I figured you were more rustlers,' he gasped. 'I was following tracks left by the herd stolen from Big T last night and got too close to the thieves. They spotted me and I had to light out fast. I'm on my way back to Big T to get the outfit.'

Benson had moved forward and was peering around a rock at the trail ahead. He drew back suddenly, pulling his gun, and called a warning.

'Two riders coming fast,' he reported.

'They're after me,' Strother said.

They prepared for the arrival of the newcomers, trailing their reins and moving up to where Benson was crouching. Stafford peered around the rock, saw the two riders and, when he judged them to be close enough, drew his gun and stepped out into the open. Harra joined him and they stood shoulder to shoulder with levelled pistols.

The riders hauled on their reins and brought their mounts to a sliding halt only feet away from Stafford and Harra. Both reached for their holstered guns despite Stafford's shouted warning.

'Hold it!' Stafford yelled.

One man threw his hands shoulder high but the other continued to make a play for his gun. Stafford's big Colt flamed and hammered, and a red splotch appeared on the man's shirt front as he pitched sideways out of his saddle. Stafford covered the survivor, who sat motionless with his hands shoulder-high.

'These are two of Polder's men,' Benson called, emerging from cover. 'That's Jake Berle with his hands in the air. He's Polder's man, for sure.'

'And one of the men who signed a statement the lawyer made that incriminated you, Benson, and some of the smaller ranchers,' Stafford mused. 'What are you doing around here, Berle, and why did you reach for your gun when you saw me?'

'I thought we had ridden into some rustlers,' the man replied. He was tall and thin, rough-looking, with piercing brown eyes that were bright and alert. 'We found the place where the rustlers are holding the stolen stock.'

'Seems like everybody today is finding that place,' Benson said. 'But you can't get away with that story,

Berle. I've seen you and Johnson in the past, herding stolen stock across the range and into the roost.'

Harra straightened from examining the other man, a grimace on his weather-beaten face. 'He's dead,' he reported.

Strother, still in Riley's grip, came forward and looked at Berle. 'I saw him with the rustlers,' he said. 'They were hazing the cattle out of the roost. Him and that dead one left the others and took out after me when I was spotted.'

'Put handcuffs on Berle, Howie,' Stafford said. 'Strother, you can ride with us if you like. Use that horse over there.'

Strother shook his head. 'I got to report back to Tudman,' he said doggedly. 'Them's my orders.'

'Well you haven't got far to ride.' Stafford smiled grimly. 'Tudman and some of the Big T crew are just behind us. Go tell him what's happened.'

Strother nodded, obviously relieved. He mounted the dead man's horse and resumed his ride down the defile, leaving a billowing cloud of dust.

'Mebbe it ain't such a good idea to let him go,' Harra mused. 'Now we've got to watch our backs as well.'

'We don't know if Big T is mixed up in the rustling.' Stafford shrugged. 'If they do attack us it will prove their guilt.'

'That's a hard way to get evidence,' Riley observed.

'Bring Berle along and keep an eye on him,' Stafford continued. He resumed the ride up the dry wash and the others followed closely.

Minutes later they reached the upper end of the defile, and Stafford reined in to look across the wide expanse of rough but fairly level ground that had opened up before them. In the middle distance a dust cloud was rolling on the breeze, and they saw the movement of many cattle heading north-east. Stafford took a small telescope from his saddle bag and raised it to inspect the distant figures. The others waited silently for his report.

'There are more than a dozen rustlers.' Stafford put away the telescope. 'I guess there's only one thing we can do. We'll go in fast and hit them hard. They're spread out all around the herd so we'll have them at a disadvantage. Make every shot count, huh? We want to break the back of this rustling, so let's move out.'

They went forward at a canter. The herd was slow-moving, and they began to overhaul it fast. As they drew nearer they could make out details, and Stafford smiled grimly when he saw a chuck wagon over to the left behind the herd. The rustlers had organized themselves down to the last detail.

'Riley, take that wagon,' Stafford said. 'Chain Berle and any prisoners to the wagon and come on after us.'

Riley grinned and veered away to the left. He had a lead rope on Berle's horse which was tied to his saddlehorn, and his sullen prisoner was forced to go along with him. Stafford kept a close watch on the rustlers but half his attention was on Riley, who reached the wagon, gun in hand, and soon overpowered the cook.

'Bill, you and Benson take the far side of the herd,' Stafford ordered. 'I'll handle this side myself. I doubt if the rustlers will give in without a fight so don't take any chances. And watch the herd. They'll stampede the instant shooting breaks out. We'll need to turn them back if they do run.'

Harra lifted a hand in acknowledgement and turned away, followed closely by Benson. Stafford checked his surroundings as he pushed his horse into a run. There were three rustlers riding drag on the herd, neckerchiefs pulled up over their lower faces to cut out the thick dust raised by the churning hoofs of the steadily-moving cattle.

One of the rustlers eventually heard the sound of approaching horses and twisted in his saddle. He immediately reached for his gun, yelling in shock at his pards, and the next instant the raucous crash of exploding six-guns hammered out the intense silence and threw strings of echoes away to the rocky horizon.

Stafford ducked instinctively as a bullet whined over his head. He palmed his pistol and threw down on the nearest rustler. The man slumped in his saddle then pitched sideways to the ground, bouncing a couple of times before lying still. Harra opened fire on the remaining two rustlers, and at that moment the cattle stampeded, turning from a sedately-walking herd into a torrent of blindly running, panic-stricken steers that poured over everything in its path like a seething brown flood. Harra's expert shooting cut down the remaining two rustlers in the drag, and harsh echoes boomed and re-echoed as dust flew in a blinding cloud.

The rustlers spaced out around the herd were alerted by the shooting, but the stampede gave them other things to think about. Harra and Benson moved down the left side of the fast flowing stream of cattle, shooting rapidly at the rustlers, taking advantage of the surprise they had created.

Stafford moved forward on the right, swapping lead with the rustlers who turned to fight. He was low in his saddle, holding his reins in his left hand while his big pistol was levelled at the distant figures. His first shot missed the nearest rustler, but when he fired again the man fell out of his saddle, to lie unmoving when Stafford galloped by.

Some of the rustlers fled without resisting, uncertain of the numbers against them. Stafford emptied his gun at them, and had the satisfaction of seeing two more drop out of the fight. Harra was having similar success on the other side of the herd, and within minutes the remaining rustlers had withdrawn.

As the gun echoes faded away, Stafford concentrated on passing the herd. He reloaded his gun as he rode, then holstered the weapon. Harra was moving up on the left, each aware of what the other intended doing. Stafford reached the lead steers, staying clear of the nodding beads with their lethal horns, and began to shoot into the ground ahead of the maddened animals.

At first his shots had no effect, but when Harra joined in on the far side the steers began to slow. Then, without warning, and as if controlled by one brain, the whole herd turned and raced back the way it had come. Riley, sitting his horse beside the chuck wagon, saw the danger of being engulfed by the thunderous hoofs, and moved swiftly to one side, taking Berle with him. Once clear, he sat his horse helplessly as the brown tide of panic-stricken beasts streamed by in an unstoppable wave.

For what seemed interminable minutes the cook was marooned on his wagon by the flooding tide that swept around him, and it seemed that he would escape catastrophe. But his team of horses suddenly lost their nerve and bolted, overturning the wagon, which soon disappeared under the flailing hoofs of the herd. The wagon was reduced to matchwood, the cook trampled underfoot, and the herd surged on until it reached the great natural basin where it had been held for weeks. The surrounding high rocks blunted the inevitable movement forward and the exhausted animals finally halted.

Stafford looked around as he followed the herd back. Harra and Benson joined him and they continued to where Riley was sitting his horse with his prisoner by his side.

'There wasn't much fight in those rustlers,' Riley said morosely. 'I expected better from them, all the talk we heard about the way they were running the county ragged. And we got company coming. Strother has got Big T with him this time.'

Stafford had already seen the half-dozen riders emerging from the draw, and he checked the loads in his gun before holstering the weapon, noting that the others did likewise as a matter of course. Then they sat in a line, waiting for Tudman to arrive. This was the perfect time for a showdown, if one was coming, and Stafford was aware of it.

# TEN

Tudman was grim of face as he reined in before Stafford. Hunched in his saddle, his knuckles were white from clenching his hands on his reins. For a moment he looked past the line of three deputies confronting him and gazed at the seething mass of cattle.

'There must be a thousand head of stock in there!' he exclaimed, his voice shaking with excitement. 'And the rustlers were moving them out when you hit them?'

'They were on the move,' Stafford admitted. 'We caught them just right. What's your position in this, Tudman?'

'How do you mean?' The rancher squared his shoulders. 'Hell, you're suspicious of me! Have you got a notion that my outfit might have been riding herd on these steers up here?' He laughed harshly but there was no mirth in his tone. 'Is that why you didn't want any of my crew riding with you?'

'We're feeling our way forward in this,' Stafford

replied. 'At the moment I don't trust anyone but my deputies. If you are innocent then I'll apologize to you later, but right now I want the downed rustlers brought together and identified, if possible. They might lead us to the man running this rustling.' He paused and considered for a moment. 'We already have a prisoner, and we'll see what questioning him turns up.'

Tudman's gaze swivelled to the sullen-faced Jake Berle and his lips thinned. 'He's Polder's man. Was put in on a small ranch that Polder heisted from one of his recent victims. I reckon Benson has told you all about that, huh? So what has Berle got to say? Has he admitted rustling on Polder's orders?'

'Leave the law dealing to me,' Stafford rasped. 'Get your men to bring in those dead and wounded rustlers. I want to put the blame squarely where it belongs, and act on the evidence before word of this gets out across the range.'

Tudman nodded and gave instructions to his men. He remained in front of Stafford while the cowpokes went over the route the herd had taken, collecting loose horses and loading them with dead rustlers.

'You can drive this herd back down to your range and hold it there until it can be sorted out,' Stafford informed Tudman. 'I've seen several different brands. We'll notify the owners and they can collect their stock. It looks like we've broken the back of the rustling, but I want the organizers.'

'I saw some more of Polder's men among the

rustlers,' Benson said. 'And there are a couple I've seen riding for M Bar. They got away when the shooting started.'

'Have you seen any of my men here?' Tudman demanded.

Benson shook his head. 'No. And I can't figure this out. How come men from different range crews are riding together? If one of the bigger ranchers was heading the stealing then he'd use his own crew to do it.'

'I've come across this thing before,' Stafford said. 'It would be a giveaway for a rancher to use his own crew. But it's a simple matter to hire a bunch of thieves and get them to join different outfits, bringing them together only when they are stealing. I guess there's someone in the background holding the reins of this operation, and he's the man I want to smoke out before news of this gets across the range.'

'Have you got any idea who could be at the back of it?' Tudman demanded.

Stafford shook his head. 'I'm a stranger on this range. But I have heard talk that you suspect Chuck Martin, and he figures it could be you.'

'I haven't changed my mind any about M Bar.' Tudman shook his head. 'But I think you've got the guilty kingpin in jail.'

'Griff Polder.' Benson stepped down from his saddle. 'I guess we oughta question Berle about that. He should know some of the answers. We caught him up here with the herd.'

'We also caught Strother up here,' Stafford

observed. 'He's your range boss, Tudman. Did you send him out to track your rustled stock?'

'I don't need to give Strother orders. He knows what has to be done and goes out and does it with no questions asked. He gives the orders around my spread.'

Stafford saw that the Big T riders were coming back, leading horses loaded with bodies. He was satisfied with the way events had developed, and pleased with the results. But a number of important questions were set in his mind, and he needed answers to them before he could finish his investigation with any satisfaction.

The riders came up and dead men were dragged from the saddles and laid in a row on the hard ground. Both Benson and Tudman walked along the silent line, looking at set faces and calling out the names of those they knew. Men who had ridden for Martin or Polder were recognized, but there were none who had been on Tudman's payroll. But that did not necessarily clear Tudman, and that thought was uppermost in Stafford's mind as he signalled for Riley to bring Jake Berle across.

Berle was sullen, uncommunicative, and gazed at the dead rustlers with downcast eyes. Stafford watched him for some minutes, but the rustler would not meet his gaze.

'You're in a lot of trouble, Berle,' Stafford said at length. 'Polder is in jail. I arrested him last night.'

Berle looked up then, and Stafford saw fear in the man's dark eyes.

'What did you arrest him for?' Berle growled.

'I haven't figured out all the charges yet, but right now I've got enough to keep him behind bars for a long time – him and anyone who works for him. So what have you got to say for yourself? You're in this up to your neck. We've got you dead to rights.'

'I ain't got a thing to say.' Berle shook his head. 'I was just doing my job. I work for Polder as a ranch boss, and if he's been getting up to no good then that's got nothing to do with me.'

Stafford turned away. He looked at Tudman. 'I'm holding you responsible for getting this herd down to your open range and holding it until the different brands are sorted out. And get a wagon up here for these bodies. I want them brought into town soon as you can make it. We'll take Berle along with us and try to run down more of the rustlers on our way back to town.'

'You can rely on me,' Tudman said harshly. 'The rest of my outfit should be on their way here. I left word back at the ranch for them to follow my tracks. We can handle this end of it.'

Stafford nodded and swung his horse. He rode away with his deputies, following the direction the herd had been taking before the surviving rustlers ran off. Riley was leading the sullen Berle. They reached the spot where they had turned the herd, and Stafford looked around for the tracks of any of the rustlers who had fled in the direction he intended taking.

'Head back to Concho by the quickest trail,

Benson, ' he said. 'We've done all we can out here. Now's the time to begin making the charges stick.'

They set out at a lope, their horses tired but willing. Stafford noted two sets of tracks leading away from the herd, left by horses moving fast across the rough ground and apparently heading for Concho. He drew Harra's attention to the prints, for Harra was expert at following sign.

Harra dismounted and studied the tracks for some time, then remounted, nodding as he rode in beside Stafford. 'I'll know these tracks anywhere now,' he said. 'Looks like they're making for town.'

Stafford glanced around, squinting his eyes at the sun, now well past its zenith. 'What time do you figure to reach town, Benson?' he asked the rancher.

Benson grimaced. 'Mebbe as the sun goes down,' he replied.

They rode through the afternoon, pausing often to rest their weary horses, and the sun was low in the western sky when they emerged from the hills and spotted Concho sprawled out before them. Reining in, they gave their mounts a breather, and Harra pointed to tracks in the earth.

'Those two rustlers made it all the way,' he observed.

Stafford nodded. 'When we reach town you better go to the livery barn and check out the horses. Find the animals wearing the shoes that left these prints, and then find the men who rode them in. We need them behind bars.'

Harra nodded, and they went on. Shadows were

creeping into the town when they finally reached it, and Stafford was pleased to see a new window installed in the law office when he dismounted outside. Riley dragged Berle out of his saddle and bundled him inside the office. Stafford stood for a moment on the sidewalk, looking around. Night was closing in, and he watched Harra disappearing into the gloom as the man went on along the street to the stable. He motioned for Benson to stay with him and they entered the law office.

Walt Sand was sitting at the desk in the office, and reached for the cell keys as he got to his feet. Stafford made a report of their trip and Sand grinned as he led the way into the cells.

'I've had a boring day,' he remarked. 'You sure cleaned out the lawless faction before you left. And I ain't had one case of gun-carrying inside of town limits. The prisoners have been as good as gold, and even the lawyer has stayed away after I threatened to put him behind bars. I've been taking statements from the prisoners, but no one is ready to spill the beans about what's been going on around here. The only thing that happened was Chuck Martin coming in this afternoon to report losing half a dozen horses yesterday, no doubt stolen by the rustlers.'

Stafford went to the door of Polder's cell. The saloonman was lying on his bunk, apparently disinterested in what was going on around him. Stafford informed him of the incidents that had taken place with the rustlers.

'Here's Jake Berle,' Stafford ended, grasping the

rustler's arm and dragging him forward. 'So what was your ranch foreman doing with the rustlers?'

'I'm not responsible for the actions of anyone who works for me,' Polder rasped. 'I trust my foremen to do their jobs according to the letter of the law. I can't tell you anything.'

'Berle ain't inclined to talk either,' Stafford smiled. 'But a couple of days in jail might loosen his tongue. I've got witnesses who are willing to testify that a number of men in your employ have been handling the stolen herds. When we've got all the evidence checked out we'll have a good case against you. Think it over, Polder. You can only help yourself by telling the truth about this business.'

The saloonman turned his back on them and Stafford walked away. There was time enough in which to produce a case against Polder.

'My two deputies showed up a short time ago,' Sand said as he locked the cell block door. 'They're keeping an eye on the town. I want to know if there's any trouble coming our way.'

'We'll get a bite to eat and then clean up,' Stafford said. 'It's been a tough day. You can expect some of Tudman's outfit to show up later, bringing in the rustlers we killed.'

'The undertaker has been burying bodies all afternoon,' Sand responded. He glanced towards the door as it was thrust open.

Stafford turned quickly, dropping a hand to his gun butt. Chuck Martin came into the office, followed by a couple of his men. Stafford was quick to note that none of them was wearing a gun.

'It's about time you showed up,' the M Bar rancher snapped. 'I've been cooling my heels around here for a couple of hours when I could have been better employed looking for the rustlers.'

'You can forget about the rustlers,' Stafford replied.

'Forget about them?' Martin's face tightened as he clenched his teeth. 'I'm losing stock all ways to the middle, and you tell me to forget about the rustlers. I've even had six horses stolen from my home pasture.'

'So I heard.' Stafford nodded. 'When were they stolen?'

'Sometime yesterday. I heard about it around noon today from one of my riders, and came straight into town to report the theft.'

'I saw two horses with M Bar brands on them in Tudman's front yard,' Stafford said easily, watching Martin's face. 'Both were dead. Shot down with the men riding them. The men were attacking Big T with a party of rustlers. Is that why you've come in to report stolen horses?'

'Are you figuring that I know something about the rustling?' Martin countered. 'It's too much to take! I'm losing stock, and being accused of rustling.'

'I'm not making accusations, just trying to get to the bottom of this business,' Stafford said. 'We caught up with the rustlers this afternoon and shot the hell out of them. We got back about one thousand head of cattle, and Ben Tudman has his outfit moving the herd down to his range, where they'll be sorted out.'

'You've got the cows back!' Martin grinned, his anger evaporating instantly. 'That's the best news I've heard in a long time. And Tudman was helping you. Were any of my brand in the herd?'

'Yeah, and some of your riders were among the dead rustlers.'

Martin jerked as if he had been struck in the face. He stared at Stafford for some moments. 'Some of my crew?' he demanded. 'Can you put names to them?'

At that moment the street door was jerked open and Bill Harra entered. He nodded at Stafford.

'What did you find, Bill?' Stafford demanded.

'Those two horses we tracked into town.' Harra spoke grimly. 'They were in the stable. And both are branded M Bar. The stableman described the men who rode in. They were only thirty minutes ahead of us. I looked in the saloons on my way here, and spotted both men in one of them.'

'Riding my horses!' Martin growled. 'They'll be two of those animals that were stolen yesterday.'

'Let's go brace the two men who rode them in,' Stafford suggested. 'We might be getting somewhere at last. You can come with us, Martin. But your two men will remain here.'

'That suits me.' Martin silenced the protests of his men with a curt motion of his right hand. 'Stay here like you're told,' he rapped.

Stafford, flanked by Harra and Riley, left the

office and walked along the boardwalk. Martin followed closely, sided by Ira Benson, and Harra moved ahead to lead the way into the saloon. There were a dozen men inside. Harra went to two men standing at the bar slightly apart from the other patrons.

'These two fit the descriptions given to me by the stableman as having ridden in on those horses,' he said. 'And they're carrying guns.'

Both men turned swiftly, hands jerking to their guns. Stafford had already palmed his pistol and was covering them.

'You two are rustlers,' he accused. 'We saw you riding away from the stolen herd and followed your tracks right into town.' He glanced at Martin. 'Are these men on your payroll?'

Martin shook his head. 'Never seen them before. Just what is going on? Where did you two get my horses from?'

Neither man replied, and Stafford shrugged.

'Let's get back to the jail,' he said. 'These two can sweat behind bars for a spell. They'll soon start talking when they see the set-up against them.'

'I've seen both these men riding around the range,' Benson said, 'trailing cattle towards that basin where we found the rustled stock. I got a good look at the herds they were driving, and there were several brands amongst them.'

Stafford grinned. 'That'll do to bring charges against them. Let's get back to the jail.'

The two men were disarmed and conveyed to the

law office. Stafford's mind was picking over the salient points of the rustling but he still could not decide who was behind it. Some evidence pointed to Chuck Martin, but he was still doubtful about Ben Tudman. He could not overlook the fact that three of Tudman's men had tried to kill him the night before.

Night had closed in and shadows lay densely over the town as they went along the sidewalk to the law office. Stafford walked at the rear of the group with Benson at his side. He maintained a close watch on Chuck Martin. Riley and Harra were escorting the prisoners, both with drawn guns. As they reached the jail Stafford heard the sound of perhaps a dozen horses coming through the darkness from out of town. He paused, aware that it was too soon for Tudman to be bringing in the dead rustlers.

'Hurry up and get those prisoners behind bars,' he rapped as Riley paused with the office door half-open. 'Then get out here, quick. This could be trouble coming at us.'

Riley and Harra moved fast, thrusting the prisoners into the law office. Sand, inside at the desk, sprang up and drew his gun, covering the prisoners, and both deputies turned in the open doorway as riders began to appear indistinctly along the street. A dozen horses slowly materialized, and Stafford reached for his holstered gun as they halted.

'Who are you?' Riley's booming voice hurled a profusion of echoes around the silent street. 'Declare yourselves, and be quick about it.'

'We need the law,' came the strident reply.

'We are the law,' Harra replied. 'What's your trouble?'

A gun flashed from among the assembled riders, and as the report rang out a bullet thudded into the front of the jail, barely missing Chuck Martin. The M Bar rancher hurled himself to the sidewalk. Stafford dropped to one knee as Riley and Harra separated and ducked out of the office doorway. Benson remained at Stafford's side, crouching as he drew his gun.

The next instant all the riders were shooting wildly, emptying their guns at the law office. Stafford narrowed his eyes and aimed at gun flashes, ignoring the crackling lead that flew around him. He could see the shapeless mass of men and horses and fired into their midst, teeth clenched, gun hand steady. Some of the riders were already spilling out of leather, and the thunderous racket of blasting guns sent raucous echoes across the darkened town.

Pausing to reload, Stafford found Martin clawing at his arm.

'I'm not armed,' the M Bar rancher yelled. 'Gimme a gun.'

Stafford shook the rancher off and resumed firing. Riderless horses went galloping by along the street. Riley and Harra were firing rapidly, and Walt Sand had come to the door of the office to snipe at the riders standing their ground.

The shooting seemed to go on endlessly, but then ceased as suddenly as it had begun. Stafford was reloading for the second time when he realized that there were no more targets. Those riders who were still in their saddles had turned and ridden off into the night. There were eight or nine motionless figures sprawled in the thick dust of the street, and an uneasy silence settled as the gun echoes faded.

'Bill, you and Howie move out to the right and cover us,' Stafford yelled. 'I want to check those men down in the street. Be ready for another attack.'

Both deputies arose instantly and moved away into the darkness. Walt Sand emerged from the law office, gun in hand and holding a lighted lantern.

'Benson,' the town marshal rapped. 'Cover those two prisoners in the office.'

Benson stepped into the doorway of the office, gun uplifted, and Sand crossed the sidewalk. Stafford carried his gun in his hand as they walked the few yards to where the foremost of the men lay, and a pang stabbed through him when the yellow rays of the lantern fell upon the upturned face of Ben Tudman, who was still gripping a pistol in his right hand although he was unconscious. A red splotch on Tudman's shirt front showed where he had taken a slug. Stafford gazed at the Big T rancher's ashen features, trying to work out what had led the man to this end. Little things were beginning to add up in his agile mind, but he needed time to think it out. He checked Tudman while Sand went to look at the other men, and was relieved to find that the rancher was still very much alive. Evidence was still needed, and if

Tudman could be induced to talk the proof would come of its own volition.

'Can I come and look over the wounded?' Doc Wilson called from the shadows across the street. 'I turned out as soon as I heard the shooting.'

'Sure. Come and do your stuff, Doc.' Stafford straightened as the doctor came to his side. 'I need Tudman alive. Do what you can to save him.'

A cooling breeze came along the street, stirring the dust and dissipating the lingering gunsmoke. Stafford heaved a sigh as tension drained out of him. Tudman's attack on the law had given him enough evidence to pin the guilt where it belonged. He suddenly realized that he was ravenous, and the eating house would be closed. But, in view of what had gone on in the past twenty-four hours, he thought Bob Carmody might stretch a point just this once and feed some hungry lawmen.

He realized that he was instinctively reloading his pistol, and holstered the weapon with a slick movement. It might not be all over yet. But he was ready for anything as he savoured the peacefulness now existing, aware that the townsmen were already emerging to check on the situation. He sighed heavily, sensing that the shooting was finally over and all that remained were the pieces to be picked up.